1986

WEEK 42

EMMA MCCLANE

Cover Design by Aleksa Luh
Content and Copy Edit by Ginny Glass

Printed in the United States of America
First Printing, 2016
ISBN: 978-91-983676-0-7
ISBN: 978-91-983676-1-4 (e-book)

www.emmamcclane.com
www.twitter.com/emmamcclane
www.instagram.com/emmamcclane

Thank you to my lovely family, friends and the awesome people in the Glamlands community on Instagram.
And sorry Lisa, for not being able to bring up your love, Sebastian Bach.

MONDAY

October 13, 1986

Resting her back against the flamingo-pink ceramic wall, Samantha moved her lips closer to the window and watched as the fresh ocean air took care of the smoke coming out of her seventeen-year-old lungs. Her blood-red lipstick stained her cigarette as she repeatedly placed it between her lips.

"How did it go with Chris over the weekend?" Julia asked as she admired her newly-bleached hair in the mirror while contributing to the tainted air of smoke and Christian Dior's Poison perfume that circulated in the high school bathroom.

"I ended it," Samantha said and shrugged like it was no big deal.

"How long did it last this time? A month?" Karen asked, deeply inhaling from her cigarette as she unzipped her black leather jacket. "Must be a record."

Their conversation was interrupted when the creaking sound of the door behind them crept into their ears and stole their attention. Entering the smoke-clouded bathroom was Clarice, a girl with long, perfectly teased, chocolate-brown hair and big, bright eyes.

Samantha moved away from the window and looked up and down Clarice's sun-kissed body. Clarice was dressed in an oversized, apricot-colored sweater with rolled-up sleeves, plain black tights, and a pair of dirty white sneakers.

"Having trouble finding the stall or what?" Karen asked to break the silence as she looked at Clarice.

Clarice rolled her eyes at Karen and started to walk toward the sinks. On her way, she looked down at the gray stone floor and giggled.

"And what are you laughing at?" Samantha asked.

"Nothing much," Clarice said and turned on the tap water. "It's just funny to see how you totally look like triplets with your matching blonde hair and leather outfits."

"Like you're so unique yourself," Julia said.

Looking over Clarice's shoulder, Samantha noticed another intruder heading in their direction through the door's cracked, rectangular window. Out in the corridor stood Mr. Morgan, glaring at Samantha, his nostrils flaring in anger, showing how he clearly smelled the scent of smoke. Samantha met his gaze and sighed as she rolled her eyes away from Mr. Morgan. She was once again caught in the act, but she did not hand out any free passes.

"I need more hairspray," Samantha said as she saw how Mr. Morgan moved closer to the door. "Hold this." She handed over her cigarette to Clarice.

"I'm not gonna hold your stinking cigarette," Clarice said and held it in front of Samantha so she could take it back.

"I am so tired of this," Mr. Morgan said as he shoved the door open with his fist and entered the toxic room.

Turning around, Clarice looked at Mr. Morgan with resignation. To her there was no point in explaining away the smoking cigarette between her small fingers, poisoning his and everybody else's airways. Just by being two steps away from Samantha Harries, Clarice was guilty by association.

Mr. Morgan was, as always, looking rather tired, with huge bags underneath his eyes, although they were barely visible through the gray, bushy eyebrows growing on the lower part of his wrinkly forehead. In the bathroom light, he looked even older than the brown, vintage Scottish blazer he wore every Monday.

"You all get detention," he said after a loud sigh and

turned his back against the girls. After a few very quiet seconds, he left the four senior students just as he had found them: annoyed and late for class.

The look Samantha got from Clarice was sharp and could have probably killed any living object within a hundredth of a second. Instead of responding with an even harsher look, Samantha just grinned at Clarice as she took back her cigarette and dumped what was left of it underneath the running tap water.

"See you in detention," she said, in her grating voice, and left the bathroom alongside Karen and Julia.

* * *

"What took you so long?" Clarice's best friend, Amanda, whispered as she leaned over to the desk on her right, where Clarice sat down after arriving six minutes late to English class.

"I ran into some trouble," Clarice answered as her whole face tightened up.

"Lucky for you, you're Mrs. Howell's favorite student," Amanda said as she watched how Mrs. Howell took back the attention of the class after Clarice's late arrival.

"Yeah, but unfortunately I'm not Mr. Morgan's favorite student at the moment."

"You can't blame yourself for that. He hates everybody

under fifty."

"True."

Opening up her English book, Clarice was ready to take in the information coming out of Mrs. Howell's mouth, but Amanda wanted more details from Clarice.

"So what kind of trouble are we talking about? Rockers?" Amanda asked discreetly in the back of the classroom and moved her curly, brown hair from one side of her shoulder to the other.

Clarice nodded her head and tried to stay focused on Mrs. Howell's grammar briefing as the thoughts of detention hammered her mind. Her parents would not be too happy if they found out, or even worse, if Mr. Morgan called them, she would not be able to give her side of the story.

"Great, now first tell me what they did to you and then what you have in mind as revenge."

Clarice gave up. As usual, Amanda was impossible to shut up unless she had all the latest information, and if Clarice still wanted a shot at an English education, it was best just to tell her right away.

"Mr. Morgan caught me holding Samantha Harries' cigarette and gave me detention," she whispered.

"What the hell were you doing with Samantha Harries?" Amanda asked louder than Clarice had wished for, which made the whole class turn around facing them.

"Amanda, do you have something you would like to

share with the entire class?" Mrs. Howell asked, as she turned around from her blackboard and stared into Amanda's eyes.

Clarice slowly leaned away from the crime scene and cuddled up against the wall in an attempt to make herself invisible.

"No, I wouldn't say I do," Amanda answered as she straightened her back and looked back down at her English book.

"Good. Then please wait until class is over to spill your latest gossip," Mrs. Howell said and continued to write another noun on the board.

Before Clarice had had a chance to read the new word on the board, she had a note laying on the open page of the book in front of her. Of course, it was from Amanda.

Plz continue!!

Clarice took out a pen out of her pink pencil case and wrote back.

I met her in the bathroom, but what is important here is my revenge plan. Don't you think she would enjoy seeing the theater group perform this afternoon?

Amanda looked at the note just like she looked at her

equations in math—like a big question mark.

And how do you think you'll succeed with that since literally all the rockers are going to L.A. this afternoon for Bon Jovi's album signing?

"Exactly," Clarice pronounced with only her lips and waggled her eyebrows.

It was obvious from the look on Amanda's face that she had no idea what Clarice was talking about, but after a short while, the muscles started to let go of the questioning wrinkles in her forehead.

Genius!! But how are you gonna stop half the school from leaving Long Beach?

As I said, I have a plan, Clarice wrote.

"Oh, wait. Let me guess. Does it involve guns and cops, just like last year?" Amanda whispered.

Clarice said no more. She said enough by being silent.

* * *

The tension between the rockers and poppers was way out of control as they all entered the auditorium after the visitation from the county police. A few rockers with anger problems now started kicking down chairs as well as knocking over both teachers and poppers. Four girls stood in the corner with broken teenage hearts and tears running down their faces.

"I can't believe we have to wait three months now before we get to see Jon's handsome face," one of the crying rockers said as she sat down on the floor to catch her breath after crying rivers.

Being searched for possession of weapons instead of attending a signing for the biggest rock album of the year was not exactly the rockers' definition of 'fun'. It did not take a genius for them to figure out that this was orchestrated by a popper, a very evil one.

Clarice was quite proud of her work. Leaving an anonymous tip to the principal about weapon rumors at school always held every student on school property until the police had searched every corner and person. As the principal walked up on stage to once again inform all the students about how bad weapons were, another rocker threw his history book up and hit one of the spotlights, which destroyed it, and glass decorated the floor and stage like shiny, sharp snowflakes.

"You and me are gonna have a little talk after this," the principal said through the microphone and pointed at the rocker.

Even though Clarice was the one responsible for this madness, she was almost happy to have detention just to have a valid excuse to leave.

As she entered Mr. Moran's geography classroom which had the big red detention sign hanging on the door, Clarice watched as Mr. Morgan leaned against his desk and Julia, Karen, and Samantha sat in the back by the window, drawing on their desks.

"Welcome to detention, Clarice," Mr. Morgan said. "Please take a seat."

The evil looks from the triplets in the corner made Clarice shiver. She sat on the desk right next to the door to keep the most distance possible.

"Okay, girls, you four are the only ones in trouble today, and I have an assignment for you," Mr. Morgan said as he placed his large grandpa-style glasses on the tip of his chubby nose. "Karen and Julia, I want you two to go into the study room and write down thirty reasons why smoking is bad, and I want Samantha to come over here and sit next to Clarice."

Samantha did not even blink, although Mr. Morgan said her name loud enough to hear. Her dreamy eyes were too busy admiring the Van Halen logo engraved in her old and dirty desk.

"Samantha!" Mr. Morgan repeated.

Samantha shifted her focus and got up from the desk with a loud sigh. The room was silent except for the sound of her knee-high leather boots clicking in time to the rhythm of the wall clock. She walked to the front desks, pulled out a chair next to Clarice's, and sat down. Throwing daggers with her eyes at Mr. Morgan, who stood in front of her, Samantha could smell the mixture of aftershave and old man. It made her head spin.

"Girls, I am well aware you don't get along," Morgan started. "To solve this issue, I have come up with an assignment for you."

The word 'assignment' made Samantha yawn, and she did not bother to hide it from Mr. Morgan as he was about to add details about the task.

"During this week, I want you two to spend some time together after school and get to know each other. By ten o'clock next Monday, I expect a handwritten report on my desk where you describe who the other person really is," Mr. Morgan said as he leaned over the girls' desks and looked deep into their eyes. "And this is a serious assignment," he added before taking a few steps back.

"If you seriously think I would spend my free time with a popper, you are way wrong," Samantha said.

"I agree," Clarice said.

Mr. Morgan inhaled loudly and sat behind his desk that was covered with piles of paper.

"If you do not complete this task, I will have no other choice but to suspend you," he said.

With the information, Samantha threw her head back and

sighed even louder than she had the time before.

"Well, I have dance class later, so I can't hang out," Clarice said.

"That is perfect," Mr. Morgan said. "I will give you permission to leave in time if you take Samantha with you."

Samantha's head fell down on the desk in front of her, and Clarice was about to do the same, but instead she started to stare into the bookshelf standing alongside the wall in front of her. To control her frustration, she began to count the number of books on the shelf. She landed on the number seventy-eight before she was interrupted by Julia and Karen as they came out of the study room in the back.

"Mr. Morgan, we've finished," Karen said as she waved with their paper in the air on why smoking is bad.

"Give me the paper, and then you may leave in silence," Mr. Morgan said, as he massaged his eyebrows with his thumb and ring finger.

Samantha looked over at Karen and Julia as they put their leather jackets back on, quickly fixed their hair, and walked with proud steps through the desks to Mr. Morgan's desk where they handed in their paper before leaving Samantha alone with Clarice in the empty classroom.

"Why didn't they have to hang out with a popper?" Samantha asked.

"Will you all please stop with the popper-rocker thing?" Mr. Morgan said, looking up from a test he was correcting.

"You two did not even go to this school when that all started, so how come it's still a thing?"

"You didn't answer my question," Samantha said.

"I promise you that time after time I will make more students get to know each other before hating one another based on what kind of music they like, but you two are my little guinea pigs," he said and looked back down at the geography test in front of him.

* * *

"Where is your fancy car?" Clarice asked as they headed for the school's parking lot after detention.

"It's at the garage," Samantha said. "But you can usually find a cab near 7-Eleven."

"Well, I think we'll manage—it's not far," Clarice said and started walking away from the school's property, but Samantha did not follow.

"Excuse me, but have you seen the shoes I'm wearing?"

"Yeah, Gucci's fall season boots in real leather. I saw them in *Vogue* a few months ago," Clarice said.

Samantha raised her eyebrows and watched as Clarice walked further and further away from her. When Clarice reached the sidewalk, Samantha finally started walking after her. It took a while for Samantha in her Gucci boots to catch up with Clarice in her Reebooks, but when she was just a few steps behind, Clarice put on her headphones and pressed play on her Walkman. Because of the extreme volume, Samantha could hear the intro to "I Wanna Rock" by Twisted Sister playing through Clarice's headphones.

"What the hell is this?" Clarice screamed as she threw off her headphones right after she put them on.

"Oh, that's a good one," Samantha said with flirty eyes. "It's Twisted Sister."

"Did you put this in here?" Clarice asked and took out the Twisted Sister cassette that had replaced her beloved Cyndi Lauper tape.

"Do you really think I would give my Twisted Sister cassette to you for free?"

"Well, somebody did," Clarice said and threw the cassette in the trash can.

"It was probably Ricky since you replaced his gym shirt with a Madonna one at PE last week."

"True," Clarice said. "And I'll get him back for this. Even harder if I don't get my Lauper album back."

"Don't count on it since you just threw away his TS cassette," Samantha said and laughed.

Coming into town, the streets were busy as usual at four o'clock. Middle-aged men and women dressed in suits were eager to get home to their families and avoid the upcoming rush hour traffic. Party-seeking college students mingled out in the street, wearing neon beachwear while having a smoke on their afternoon breaks from work. The dance studio was located right next to Long Beach's most popular gym, where people came in and out like some sort of clothing store. The gym had a perfect view of the ocean because of its huge, open windows, and the people walking on the street had a just as good view of the people with sweaty, glowing skin, spending their Monday afternoons on spinning bikes.

"Look at them," Samantha said and pointed at the people working out by the window. "How can they?"

"You mean work out? I think it is pretty fun," Clarice said.

"It is probably the most boring thing ever next to homework and *Miami Vice*," Samantha said.

Clarice could not help but laugh while she opened the door to the dance studio.

"You can place your shoes here," Clarice said, as she put her Reebooks in the shoe rack by the door.

"Oh, great, you're here," Clarice's dance teacher, Daisy, said as she saw Clarice coming down the hallway.

Dressed in white leggings and a brownish-green-colored bodysuit, with her blond hair tied up in a bun, Daisy looked at Samantha, whom she had never seen before.

"Daisy, this is Samantha, and unfortunately, she will be joining us today," Clarice said.

"What do you mean? Don't we love having guests in our class?" Daisy said as she greeted Samantha with a smile and a strong handshake. "I'm Daisy, and I teach this class as a part of my college course."

"How exciting," Samantha said sarcastically as she shook Daisy's hand.

"She needs to borrow some clothes," Clarice added as she watched how Samantha was seconds away from exploding with irritation.

Without saying a word, Daisy led the girls into a small storage room behind the pink door on the right side of the hallway. She opened a box standing on the floor and gave Samantha a few colorful clothing items.

"You can change in here if you'd like, or you can go down the corridor to the left where you'll find a proper changing room," Daisy said.

Samantha looked up at the shelves filled with boxes in the room and slowly shook her head. She seemed kind of nervous and lost, which to Clarice was understandable, considering the circumstances. Samantha closed the door to the storage room where she would change in private.

"See you in the studio," Daisy said to Clarice as she walked further down in the corridor.

When Samantha walked out of the storage room, she was wearing shiny blue tights, a yellow bodysuit with a thong up to her hips, white leg warmers, and a pink scrunchie. That was the cherry on top to keep her long bleached-blonde hair away from her pretty face. Clarice had never seen anything more shocking in her life. It was hilarious.

"You have never looked better," Clarice said with a big laugh.

"Oh, shut up."

"Why did you even agree to this?" Clarice asked, for once interested in what Samantha had to say for herself.

"Because if I get suspended ever again, my awful parents will destroy my music collection, and if I have to dress up like this to save it, then so be it," she said and walked toward the studio.

Clarice followed Samantha down the hall and took off her sweater on the way. Underneath, she was wearing a bright blue top, and from her sports bag, she took a pair of pink legwarmers to add over her tights.

"Good afternoon, class," Daisy said after Clarice and Samantha had shut the door behind them and placed themselves on a free spot in the room. "Today we'll start off by warming up to last week's choreography for "Wake Me Up before You Go Go"."

She got down on her knees by the mirrors in front of the class and placed Wham's *Make It Big* album from 1984 into the stereo. As she pressed play, the speakers sang out the famous jitterbug tones of the song, and Daisy rolled her shoulders back and forth before getting into position. As the song went on, Samantha did nothing but watch Daisy and all the other girls in the room snap their fingers and spin around in circles. She was paralyzed.

"Come on. Let's move it," Clarice said when looking over at Samantha.

Samantha let out a sigh and carefully started to move to the rhythm by clapping her dead-fish hands. She moved her hips around and followed the other girls as they now and then raised their arms up and got down on their knees.

"What's the point in wearing leg warmers?" Samantha asked as she started to feel the uncomfortable heat from her calf. "This is California. It's probably like seventy-eight degrees outside."

"It helps the blood circulation and smooths the muscles," Clarice said while doing a high kick.

By the end of the song, sweat was visible on some of the girls. But there was no time to rest since Daisy jumped right into the next dance routine set to "Footloose" by Kenny Loggins.

"I know him," Samantha said.

"You know Kenny Loggins?" Clarice asked.

"No, Kevin Bacon from the movie. He and my brother went to theater class together."

"That's bangin'," Clarice said and smiled.

* * *

The sun was still shining brightly over the horizon as Samantha and Clarice walked out from the dance studio after class at half past five. Clarice threw her neon-green bag over her tanned shoulder and asked Samantha how she would get home.

"I'll probably take a cab," Samantha said and sprayed some extra hairspray on her hair while looking through a tiny makeup mirror. "How about you?"

"I'm meeting a friend at the diner around the corner," Clarice said as she pointed at the intersection behind them.

"Okay then, see you tomorrow when I get to decide what you'll be doing with your afternoon," Samantha said.

"Aren't you gonna ask me something first?"

Samantha turned around to face Clarice with her confusion.

"What do you mean? Do you want me to ask you to the prom or something?"

"No, but we are here together for a reason," Clarice said. "And that is to get to know each other, so maybe you should ask me something before we split."

"I already know plenty about you," Samantha said. "Your name is Clarice, you are seventeen years old, you were probably born and raised here in California, and you want to be a journalist after graduation."

Clarice wrinkled her forehead as she looked into Samantha's green eyes.

"How do you know I want to be a journalist?"

"You wrote it in some essay that I stole from Mrs. Hopkins' desk and read through before I kinda burned it," Samantha said and tried to keep herself from laughing as she looked the other way.

Clarice tried to control herself by biting her lower lip and breathing heavily through her nose.

"Feel free to tell me more about yourself tomorrow, but now I really want to get home so I can pick up my car," Samantha said. "And can we please keep quiet about this assignment? I don't want to create unnecessary drama."

"Gladly. We don't want to end up like Matt and Celeste."

"Matt and Celeste who?" Samantha asked.

Clarice was surprised Samantha did not know about the most revolutionary love story of Long Beach High. It had been the biggest scandal of their sophomore year, and everybody had talked about it.

"Matt the popper and Celeste the rocker who had a secret love affair? Doesn't that ring a bell?" Clarice asked.

"Were they the ones who transferred 'cause they got so much hate from everybody?"

"Yes."

"Not that I would mind transferring from LBH, but yeah, let's keep quiet," Samantha said. "See ya," she added and walked away from Clarice toward the yellow taxis parked on the other side of the street.

Clarice watched as the cab Samantha stepped into headed north and went out of sight behind the supermarket around the corner. "This is gonna be interesting," she thought before she turned around and walked toward the diner.

Whistling to Bruce Springsteen's "Born in the USA", Tom stood with his back against the peach-colored stone wall outside the diner as Clarice arrived from around the corner. He looked flawless as usual, dressed in his oversized, orange blazer with a white-and-blue-striped T-shirt underneath, tucked into his light-blue, stonewashed Levi's jeans with a brown belt around his waist. His award-winning hair was the perfect ashy-brown shade and was combed back on the sides and lightly curled in front and down the back. It was how Elvis's hair would have looked like if he was still alive.

"Finally," he said, noticing Clarice's presence.

She walked up to him and let him kiss her softly on the cheek, as he always did when they met after school, before entering Fletcher's Diner. They sat down at a free booth which had a view over the beach promenade. Tom waved at the waitress and asked for 'the usual' while Clarice placed her bag next to her and took a deep breath. With its few customers, the restaurant was calm. A couple of students occupied a table further into the diner with piles of books and papers all over it while drinking milkshakes, and a few older men dressed in construction uniforms watched a hockey game on the television. The smell of freshly grilled hamburgers circulated in the air, and Clarice felt her stomach aching for food.

With a big smile at Tom, the cute, red-haired waitress placed two big sundaes on the table, topped with extra chocolate and cookie crumble.

"Thanks, Alicia," Tom said with a smile and looked deep into her eyes before she left him and Clarice alone with their ice creams.

"You are so cheesy," Clarice said while shaking her head at Tom.

"What do you mean? I'm just being friendly," Tom said.

"Whatever you say, Mr. Casanova."

Tom took a big scoop of the sundae and placed it in his mouth while looking funny at Clarice.

"So, what were you up to this weekend?" Clarice asked to start a proper conversation.

"Good question," he said. "I visited a few old friends back home in Pasadena, brought my sister to Disneyland for her birthday, and dropped in for a while at Gary's party. Why didn't I see you there?"

"Jesus, I totally forgot. How was it?"

"I can't say you missed much, but your ex was there, and it looked like he could use some attention," Tom said with amusement.

Clarice wrinkled her forehead and looked down at her

ice cream.

"It still chokes me that he's back," she said.

"Yeah, he could probably have bought himself a nice mansion back in Houston with all that contract money."

"How old is your sister now?" Clarice asked to change the subject. "Seven? Eight?"

"Eight," Tom answered with a huge amount of sundae in his mouth.

"She has gotten so big since I first met her when you moved here."

"She sure has," Tom said, "and now she wants to be a politician like Mom and Dad."

Clarice laughed and tried to keep the ice cream from falling out of her mouth.

"So your brilliant, manipulative plan to talk shit about politics didn't work out?" she asked with flirty eyebrows.

"I'm not giving up that easily. I can't have three politicians in my family, never in a million years," Tom said. "Hopefully by next week she will want to be a swim coach or something."

Clarice took the last scoop of her ice cream and leaned back against the backrest. By the TV, the construction men cheered loudly as the game ended with a win for the Long Beach Ice Dogs, as Tom went straight over to the jukebox standing in the corner to put on some music. He started playing "Down Under" by Men at Work.

"Hey, man," a Japanese twenty-year-old-something guy said and put his hand on Tom's shoulder. "Put on some Led Zeppelin, would ya?"

Tom looked over his shoulder to see the face of the guy who asked him to torture his ears with terrible music.

"Five bucks," Tom said and reached out his hand.

The Japanese raised his eyebrows and thought for a while.

"Fine," he said and grabbed five dollars from his back pocket and placed it in Tom's hand.

"Help yourself," Tom said and moved away from the jukebox. "Come on, Clarice. I'll buy you a coffee before we bounce."

"Nice. I could use one for tonight's studying," she said as she got out of the booth and walked over to the checkout.

"Alicia, can we get two coffees to go please?" Tom said.

Alicia paused the second round of milkshake making for the college students and jumped right on Tom's order.

"Of course," she said and started to blush. "Here you go. It's on me."

"You are too sweet, Alicia," Tom said taking the coffees in his hands. "See you around."

"Be sure to drop in soon," she said with a big smile.

Tom gave one of the two coffees to Clarice and waved good-bye to Alicia as the door closed behind them.

"See you in school tomorrow," Clarice said as she

leaned in to hug Tom out on the street.

"Good luck studying," Tom said as he hugged her back.

"Thanks, although I'll probably spend my time in front of MTV as usual."

"Yeah, me too," Tom said with a smile and turned around, away from Clarice as he headed for the beach promenade to get home.

Clarice took a sip of her hot coffee and opened her sports bag to find a new tape to listen to. Madonna would do, and she put on her headphones. On the way home, she danced a few discreet moves to "Like a Virgin" as she analyzed the day that was almost over. It had sure been a weird one, dance class with Samantha and all.

* * *

"Dad, please, can we go now?" Samantha asked as she tried to make herself visible in front of her father, who was talking work over the phone.

"How is the blood pressure? And how did it go with the donor?" her father asked, as he continued his conversation and leaned over the kitchen counter.

Samantha rolled her eyes and took out her impatience on her leg as she slapped it repeatedly.

"Dad, come on," she said, sounding almost as demanding as when her mother tried to take her to the dentist back in the days.

Her father finally paid attention, scratched his thin, dark-blond hair and nodded in response.

"All right, Henry, I have to go and pick up Sam's car, but I'll come in right after," he said. "Just make sure all preparations for the operation are completed." He hung up the phone.

"You're unbelievable," Samantha said and watched as her father walked closer to her and took his car keys that hung on the golden hook by the hallway mirror.

"There is a man who can die if I don't operate him tonight," he said and opened the front door. "So we'll have to be quick at the garage, and you can order takeout for dinner."

Samantha followed him down the stairs and headed for the passenger seat of the white Porsche parked just in front of the house.

"Not to sound rude, but I think there are more people in this area that can do heart surgery besides you," she said and closed the car door.

"Well, if you better your grades and go to medical school, maybe they'll call you instead of me next time," he answered and started the engine.

"For the last time, I'm not going to medical school," Samantha said. "Not law school either, for that matter."

Her father opened the top button of his black shirt and pulled down the window to let in some fresh air into the stuffy car.

"If you want to keep that Corvette of yours, you better rethink what you just said."

Samantha looked at her father from the corner of her eye and wanted to scream. Or at least jump out of the car.

"Uncle Tony gave me that car, so you can't really do anything or I'll report you to the police for theft," Samantha said.

"But I could stop paying for your gas."

"Right, so then you would have to drive me to school. I bet you can fit that into your schedule."

He laughed in order to hide his mounting irritation. He had to do that quite regularly to survive Samantha's attitude.

"I guess you'd have to take the bus then," he said and drove past the car in front of him.

"Then I wouldn't go to school. And you would be the reason," Samantha said and crossed her arms, feeling like a winner since her father couldn't possibly beat that argument. And even if he could, the look on his face said he'd had enough of this conversation.

TUESDAY

October 14, 1986

It was not until lunchtime that Clarice and Samantha saw each other again since the dance studio. Walking into the school's cafeteria, Samantha had Karen on her left side and Julia on her right. Meanwhile Clarice linked arms with Amanda as they strolled through all the red tables with rockers sitting on one side and poppers on the other.

The sun was shining brightly through the ceiling-high windows, and some students ate their lunch out on the lawn, leaning their backs on palm trees instead of sitting on each other's laps in the crowded and loud indoor cafeteria. Amanda and Clarice carried their trays with spaghetti and meat sauce from the bar and sat down by a table full of poppers who all were looking over at one of the rockers' tables.

"What's going on?" Clarice asked.

"Wait and see," Tom said.

Clarice turned her focus back to the rockers' table where three guys now sat down. All of a sudden, with a sound loud enough to scare off a group of children, the three rocker boys fell down backward to the ground with their trays flying in the air, making a perfect landing on each of their faces. Just a few seconds ago, their hairdos had been as high as the Capitol Records Building, but thanks to their Coca-Colas and spaghetti, they'd exploded like the space shuttle *Challenger*. Laughter was all around until one of the victims, dressed in ripped jeans and a Metallica T-shirt, stood up, red-faced, a vein in his temple pulsing.

"Who did this!" he screamed.

He asked again and again but did not get any answers, only more laughter. Bending down, he helped his friend up from the floor and poured another Coke over his other friend, out of irritation, before leaving the cafeteria with heavy steps.

"How did that happen?" Amanda asked while laughing.

"All right, I'll tell you the story," Tom said and sucked in a straw of spaghetti hanging outside his mouth. "Yesterday after mine and Andy's science class, Rich and Nick had spray-painted 'Andy was here' outside the classroom wall.

As we were all walking out, Mr. Gord caught Andy looking at the masterpiece and went straight to the principal's office. As punishment, he now has to assist the janitor after school hours for the rest of the week, but he came up with the clever idea to use the janitor's tools to unscrew a few pieces from Rich and Nick's lunch table as revenge."

"Are you guys talking about me?" Andy asked as he arrived after physics class and sat down next to Tom.

"The man of the day has arrived!" Tom said. "You just missed the show, but let me tell you: it was great."

"I thought I heard Nick scream," Andy said, laughing, and looked over at the bench he had ruined.

"Great job," Amanda said as she invited Andy into a high five.

He accepted her invitation and high-fived for his accomplishment. Thereafter, he started to mix his spaghetti with a ton of ketchup.

"Hey, Clarice, Brian asked me to ask you if you could help him get back at two freshmen rockers for stealing his clothes during baseball practice yesterday," Andy said while looking at Clarice with his mouth full of spaghetti.

"Typical freshmen move," Clarice said and shook her head. "Fine, I'll help, but how did he solve the problem?"

"Don't worry. I had an extra T-shirt with me, but he walked home in his baseball pants."

"You are so sweet, Andy, helping her little brother like

that," Amanda said and admired Andy's movie-star face and Rob Lowe-styled hair.

Andy responded with an excessively wide smile that showed off his cute dimples.

"Well, it was great talking to you guys, but we're watching a movie in English class, and I need to reserve a seat," Clarice said as she got up from the table. "And so do you, Amanda."

"Okay, fine," Amanda said and got up from the lunch table.

Walking out of the cafeteria, Clarice looked over at Samantha's table where she sat eating her lunch while the guy next to her stared right down her black shirt, without her noticing or disapproving. Clarice giggled discreetly to herself and continued walking toward the hallway.

As she opened up her ocean-blue locker, a note fell out and landed on the floor. It was a piece of lined notepad paper with the words, *Old bus stop, 4pm*, signed *S*.

"Secret admirer?" Amanda asked out of curiosity.

"Maybe," Clarice said and tossed the piece of paper in the black garbage can hanging next to her locker on the wall.

* * *

Looking at the school's old backyard clock, which, surprisingly, still worked, Samantha saw that the time was exactly 4pm. She got up from the bench by the bus stop and headed over to her car that was parked along the sidewalk. Just as she was about to turn the keys and leave, she saw Clarice coming around the corner through her rearview mirror.

"Are we in a rush?" Clarice asked as she walked the last few steps up to Samantha's black 1984 C4 Corvette.

"So you decided to show up after all," Samantha said.

"Oh, come on. I was like ten seconds late."

"Whatever. Get in the car," Samantha said. "But be careful. The seats are brand-new."

Clarice walked around the car that had been polished with care, like Snow White's red apple, and opened the door to the passenger seat. As she sat down, Samantha turned the keys, and Mötley Crüe's album *Shout at the Devil* started playing louder than anything Clarice had ever heard before. She covered her ears while Samantha put on her round, metal classic Ray-Ban sunglasses and hit the gas pedal.

"Where are we going?" Clarice asked loud enough to overpower Mötley Crüe.

"You'll see when we get there."

"What?" Clarice asked.

"You'll see when we get there," Samantha repeated, screaming the words since turning down the volume was not an option.

With her ears bleeding, Clarice tried to calm herself

down by closing her eyes, leaning back against the new, all-black leather seat and focused on the air flying through her hair, causing a wild hair tornado.

Samantha turned right from the main road and drove by a few cream-colored apartment buildings. She parked the Corvette outside a three-story building and turned off the engine.

"Jesus Christ," Clarice said and exhaled loudly.

"What?" Samantha asked.

"I'm just glad I made it out alive."

"I didn't go that fast," Samantha said and moved her glasses from the tip of her nose to her head.

"Didn't go that fast," Clarice said while laughing ironically. "You went like sixty miles per hour on a thirty-mile-per-hour street."

"I did not."

"You sure as hell did. But I guess you didn't hear my protests because of that loud noise you were playing."

"Gosh, you sound just like my parents," Samantha said as she took out the keys and stepped out of her car.

She looked over at Clarice, who acted as if she did not know whether to laugh or cry, but she shook her head and got out of the car as well.

"Do you live around here, or where are we?" Clarice asked as she slammed the door.

"Come on," Samantha said and started walking around

the corner of the building.

They approached a black door with a red neon sign over it that said 'Record Records' in an italic font.

"I welcome you to the best and most secretive record store in all of Long Beach," Samantha said and went up to the door to open it.

Clarice walked behind Samantha and followed her into the record store. Standing by the door, she had an overview of the entire space that basically was a basement full of music. All of the music was categorized with big colorful signs hanging from the ceiling. CDs and cassettes were placed on shelves alongside the walls, and LPs stood from *A* to *Z* in disc racks. The white walls were barely visible since they were all covered with posters of the Rolling Stones, Elvis, Michael Jackson, and much more. Clarice's stomach started to bubble out of excitement as she saw the huge section of pop music alongside the left wall and walked over immediately. Samantha went straight to the counter in the back of the store where a forty-something-year-old guy stood, cleaning a Frank Sinatra vinyl with a light-pink cloth.

"It's been a while since I saw your beautiful face around here," said the guy behind the counter.

"You know how it is during concert season, John," Samantha said and smiled. "I have to check out the bands first before I decide on buying the albums. But now I have a full list of them to hunt down."

"Awesome. May I see?" John asked.

Samantha put her hand down her back right pocket and got ahold of a yellow Post-It note full of album titles.

"I see you have a handful of goodies right here," John said while looking at the sheet and started walking toward the glam rock section.

The first album on the Post-It note was Sunset Strip's newest overnight sensation, Poison's *Look What the Cat Dragged In*. John flipped through the records behind the *P*-to-*S* tag and grabbed an album with four male faces covered in makeup and jewelry on it. They looked like actual drag queens, with thick full eyeliner and colorful lipstick painted on their pouting lips. John handed over the album to Samantha and started to look for the other records on the list.

"They don't look this harsh on MTV," Samantha said.

"Luckily not," John said. "They went a bit overboard on the album cover, but the album itself is really good."

Samantha turned the album around and looked at the set list.

"Yeah, I've heard most of these live," she said.

"Here you have your Cinderella and Ratt albums," John said and gave her two more vinyl records.

"Three down, seven to go."

John looked up from the disc racks and faced Samantha.

"Did you win the lottery or what?" he asked while laughing.

"No, I just collected a bit of cash lying around the house," Samantha answered and looked through some albums behind the *Z* tag.

John flipped through the albums fast, like a computer scan, and paused for a second when he found what he was looking for.

"Greatest album of the year, *Slippery When Wet*," he said as he held out another album.

Flipping through the pop records, Clarice looked even more excited than Samantha. After picking up Irene Cara's debut album from 1982, she just could not keep her shaking hands together. She placed it among the other three albums she had found and walked over to Samantha and John.

"How's it going?" Clarice asked.

"Very well, thank you for asking," John said and saw how Samantha rolled her eyes away from him. "Have you found anything interesting?"

"Tons," Clarice said and held out the collection she had under her arm. "Some Irene, some Hall & Oates, Madonna, and more."

"If you don't have it already, I can really recommend Peter Gabriel's album called *So*," John said.

"I love that album!" Clarice said. "I bought it on its release day. "Sledgehammer" is rad."

Samantha watched as the two people in front of her talked passionately about pop music and fake yawned at their conversation to get John's attention back.

"I only have David Lee Roth's album on cassette," John said after looking at the last album written on the list. "Is that okay?"

"Now you made me really sad, John," Samantha said. "Of course, I already have the album on both cassette and CD, but I need it on vinyl."

"Why would you need the same album in three different forms?" Clarice asked.

"Because David Lee Roth is God," Samantha said. "And just like we see God through the Father, the Son, and the Holy Spirit, David Lee Roth needs to be seen and heard in three different forms as well."

Both Clarice and John looked at each other as if Samantha was totally crazy.

"Well, then I do apologize for not being able to serve you with the third piece of God, aka 'Diamond Dave'," John said.

Samantha looked shady at John and shrugged.

"I guess nine out of ten will have to do," she said and walked back over to the counter.

"Nine vinyls for Mrs. David Lee Roth and two vinyls plus two cassettes for her friend. That will be…," John started and looked up at the ceiling while figuring out the total costs.

"Just take this," Samantha said and handed him a one-hundred-dollar bill.

Unlike Samantha, Clarice had already counted the prices of all her records and knew just what she would have to pay. With a big smile on her lips, she handed her cash to John and watched as he pushed some buttons on the cash register. He then put their albums in two separate plastic bags with the store's logo on it.

"Here you go," he said as he handed the bags to the girls over the counter.

"Thank you," Clarice said.

"You're welcome."

"You better have David's vinyl next time I enter this door," Samantha said before walking out of the store.

Breathing in the fresh air outside of the record store, Clarice felt happy about her purchase and wanted to listen to the albums right away.

"That was a nice place," Clarice said, "and so was the owner."

"He's cool," Samantha said. "He opened the store twenty years ago when he was only seventeen."

"Wow," Clarice said and grabbed the handle of the car. "Where are we going now?"

"If you want, we can go to my place. I'm home alone."

Surprised, Clarice looked over at Samantha behind the steering wheel, who just invited a popper over to her house.

"Well, that's an offer I can't turn down," Clarice said

since this was a historic event in Long Beach High history.

"I bet you can't," Samantha said as she left the parking space and headed toward the freeway.

* * *

Samantha's house was white, big, and located just by the beach. Coming up the driveway, Clarice opened her eyes widely to take in the full picture. Two palm trees grew on each side of the entrance, and rose bushes separated the garden from the street. The beach house almost looked like a palace, not a palace for royalty, but for movie stars. Its black roof matched the windowsills, and eight steps up the stairs, there was a huge, dark double door leading into the house.

"You live *here*?" Clarice asked while Samantha parked her Corvette just by the stairs in front of the house.

"Well, I wouldn't really park my car in someone else's driveway," Samantha said and stepped out of the vehicle.

Grabbing her Record Records bag from the backseat, Samantha then took out her house key from the pocket of her oversized black blazer and walked up the stairs to the door. Clarice was speechless when Samantha opened the door as she was greeted with the most beautiful ocean view she had ever seen in her life through the glass wall at the back of the house. The house was so open and bright, the complete opposite of Samantha. Standing on the doormat, Clarice saw the kitchen, located two steps down, right in front of her with the ocean view behind it. Out on the porch, there was a pool, six sunbeds, a table with two gray couches next to it, and a big, dark-blue parasol for extra sun protection.

"What do your parents do for a living?" Clarice asked with her mouth drooling.

"Mom is a lawyer in L.A., and my dad is a surgeon," Samantha said and walked down to the kitchen to grab two Cokes from the refrigerator.

"They both work in L.A.?"

"No, only Mom, but Dad works crazy hours and travels a lot, so I'm alone most of the time."

Clarice walked up to the wall by the kitchen and looked at all the pictures hanging in different-sized frames.

"What about your brother?" Clarice asked as she looked closer at an old family photo taken in front of the White House in Washington, DC. Samantha looked so cute, dressed in a pink dress with the Barbie logo on the chest with her blonde hair up in a ponytail, sitting on her brother's shoulders. Her brother looked like a typical 1970s' teenager. His ash-blond hair was thick and had volume, without the help from teasing and hairspray. He wore a blue shirt with a white little bow around his long neck.

"Well, he is ten years older than me and goes to college, like, everywhere," Samantha answered. "I'm not sure, but I think he's in Oxford now."

"I've been to England once on vacation a couple of years ago. What does he study?"

"I have no freaking clue. He did go to medical school, but now I think he plans on working for NASA or something."

The largest photo on the wall was Dr. and Mrs. Harries's wedding portrait. With Dr. Harries in a black tuxedo and Mrs. Harries in a slim-fitted white wedding dress, they looked into each other's newly wedded eyes in front of the St. Agatha church in Philadelphia back in 1961, according to the date written in the right corner. Samantha looked just like her mother in that picture. Green eyes, rosy-blushed cheeks, a perfectly defined jawline, and long platinum-blonde hair. Although Samantha's hair had a much messier finish, unlike her mother's sixties wedding 'do.

"Your parents look so young," Clarice said as she admired the beautiful wedding photo.

"They are forty-six," Samantha answered. "Not in that picture, though."

She handed over the soda to Clarice who could not stop looking at the pictures on the wall. She could not believe it was Samantha she saw in some of the photos. In her eyes, Samantha was a rebellious rocker, and in these pictures, she looked like an angel wearing sequins and Barbie dresses while joyously smiling.

"When was this taken?" she asked and pointed at a

picture with Samantha and her parents cuddling in a hammock.

"Around '73, I think, in the backyard of my childhood home in Philadelphia."

"I knew your accent wasn't Californian," Clarice said.

"So you did, huh?" Samantha said and started to walk toward the stairs up to the second floor.

Clarice had to force herself to move away from the pictures on the wall. They were so interesting.

"When did you move here?" She asked.

"I don't know, five or six years ago maybe," Samantha said. "It was when my Dad got the job at the hospital, which I believe was around 1980."

"Nice."

As Clarice followed Samantha up the stairs, she got an overview of the full kitchen, hallway, and living room with a TV, three sofas, and paintings hanging on the wall. The floors were bright and nicely polished, and the walls were all white. The upstairs area was practically a loft with four rooms—one belonging to Dr. and Mrs. Harries, one to Samantha's brother, one master bathroom, and the last one to Samantha herself. As Samantha opened the door to her own world, Clarice's mouth closed. She was back on common ground. Besides the queen-sized bed, TV, wardrobe, and record player, her room was full of posters of band members. Most of them pictured Van Halen and David Lee Roth, but

Mötley Crüe, Bon Jovi, KISS, AC/DC, and Def Leppard were also up there. Her music collection covered almost half the room, stored in two large racks against the wall. It made Clarice feel like she was back at the record store, but with no pop section. Samantha walked straight up to her bathroom door and kissed the glued-on full-size poster of David Lee Roth on the lips before she turned on MTV.

"You sure have a few eyes watching you while you sleep," Clarice said and looked around the room and all the posters.

"The best one is up there," Samantha said and pointed up at the ceiling over her bed. "It's a seven-by-five foot poster of Van Halen from their album photoshoot for *Women and Children First.*"

Clarice looked up at the huge black-and-white poster with the four members of Van Halen having a great time over Samantha's bed.

"I have a question for you," Clarice said.

"Hit it."

"If you love Dave so much, does that mean you don't like the new Van Halen with that curly-haired guy?"

"No, I like Sammy. It just isn't the same without Diamond Dave," Samantha said and opened her Record Records bag while sitting on the floor in front MTV.

"Why did you become a rocker?"

Samantha looked at the back of the Bon Jovi album she

had just purchased and flashed back to when she was fourteen years old and just a few weeks away from starting freshman year of high school.

"Well, I was flicking through a magazine to find some clothing inspiration for the start of school and came across that poster over there of David," she said and pointed at the poster just above her record player where David Lee Roth was wearing only a black leather jacket, showing off his hairy chest. "And instead of going to the mall to buy clothes, I went to a record shop and asked if they had any of Van Halen's albums, and I bought their debut album from 1978 and was completely sold from the moment I heard Eddie's guitar at the opening of "Running with the Devil"."

"Interesting," Clarice said and took the liberty of placing herself on the bed as she watched Samantha open her records like they were her stocking presents on Christmas Day.

"What about you then?" Samantha asked.

"I don't really have a specific moment like you. I was just really into music I could dance to, and preferred the poppers' fashion."

Samantha shrugged and went back to focusing on the set list of all her new albums.

The telephone rang. Clarice heard loud and clear when Samantha sighed as she got up from the floor and walked over to the bedside table to answer it.

"Yes?" Samantha said.

"Samantha, it is Julia."

"What's up?"

"I need to see you right away. I'll be at your house in five minutes."

Clarice saw how Samantha bit her lower lip as if she was in trouble or trying to solve a big problem.

"Uh, well, if it is an emergency, of course, I'll come to the hospital."

"What do you mean?" Julia asked confused over the phone.

Clarice sat up from the bed and looked at Samantha trying to figure out what was going on.

"See you there," Samantha said and hung up the phone.

"What going on?" Clarice asked.

"My uncle was in a car accident, and I need to go to the hospital. Is your place on the way?"

"If you mean the big hospital, then yes."

"Okay, let's go then," Samantha said and headed for the stairs.

* * *

Parking her car outside the hospital, Samantha saw Julia waiting on one of the benches by the main entrance.

"Why did you want to meet here?" Julia asked as Samantha walked up to her.

"My dad called about an emergency and asked me here, but it was a false alarm," Samantha said. "Now what did you want to talk about?"

"Karen is really interested in Chris," Julia said after taking a deep breath. "Like, really interested."

"That's what you wanted to talk about? I've known that since like sophomore year."

"You have?"

"I just said I have."

Julia wrinkled her forehead and crossed her arms while watching two older ladies who entered the hospital through the doors behind her.

"So you dated him even though you knew Karen had a thing for him?"

"Well, he didn't have a thing for her, so..." Samantha said. "Why are we even having this discussion?"

"She wanted me to ask you if you were over him."

Samantha laughed to herself and looked down at the pavement to keep her annoyance in check by not looking at Julia.

"Then you can go and tell her that I am over him, and wish her a happy twelfth birthday from me for sending you to ask me that question," she said and walked back to her car.

* * *

Clarice opened the door to her apartment and was greeted by a baseball thrown at her.

"Brian, Dad has told you thousands of times not to play baseball inside," Clarice said. "The park is just outside."

"I'm sorry, Clarice. It was my fault," Brian's friend Nathan said from the kitchen.

Just as Clarice took off her shoes, her father opened the door behind her and caught his son in the act.

"That's it, Brian. I won't drive you to your game in L.A next week."

"That's okay, Dad. Clarice's friend Andy said he would drive me anywhere in his new Mustang," Brian said and threw the ball back to Nathan.

"Then you are grounded."

Clarice, who had nothing to do with the conversation, escaped the crime scene and entered her room that was way too messy to enjoy. She picked up the clothes on her floor and threw them in the laundry bag. Now her beautiful wooden floor was visible again, and she took a look around the room before starting her homework.

Although Clarice's room was the smallest one in the entire apartment, she had enough space for all her stuff. She had a comfortable bed with a white headboard, a bedside table, and a TV at one end of the room and her desk, mirror, and closet in the other. She also had her own balcony furnished with a small table and two matching wooden chairs, and a whole lot of plants. In the corner, she had a miniature palm tree about the same height as her, a flower box hanging over the edge of the balcony full of wine-red flowers, and a few spices growing in pots on the small bench standing against the wall under her window.

"Clarice, the pizza is here," Clarice's stepmother said from the hallway.

"No homework for me then," she said to herself before heading toward the kitchen where she clearly smelled pizza. Hopefully, it would have extra cheese on top.

"Great to have you back, Jessica," Brian said as he sat down at the kitchen table with his big eyes on the pizza in front of him.

"You're just saying that because I buy the best pizza," Jessica said as she sat down on the other side of the table.

"Will you ever tell us where it's from?" Clarice asked.

Jessica shook her head slowly and filled the glass in front of her with water before taking a slice of the pizza.

"All right, kids, what have you been up to today?" Clarice father, Jack, asked as he dragged his hands through his hair that during the last year had become grayer and grayer.

"Me and Nathan put his bird spider in a guy's locker at school, and he freaked," Brian said.

"It was really funny," Nathan added.

Clarice looked at her little brother and his friend having

a major laughing session next to her at the table while filling their mouths with pizza.

"How did it go on your geography test today, Clarice?" Jessica asked.

"I now have proof that I know all the states," Clarice said.

"Because I am so smart and everybody loves me," Brian said, imitating his sister.

Clarice responded to her brother's comment with an overtly evil look.

"That's great, Clarice," Jack said.

"Thanks," Clarice said and took another bite of her pizza. "Are you ready for the game tomorrow?" she asked the boys, to change the subject.

"We'll definitely win this one," Nathan said. "Are you coming?"

"I don't think I'll have the time," Clarice said.

"It's just because your ex-boyfriend is our new coach," Brian said.

"No, it's not. Why would I care that he's your coach?"

Brian took a huge bite of his pizza and looked up at Clarice with his big brown eyes.

"Are you kidding me? He left you for professional baseball without saying a word, and you expect me to believe that you're over that?" he said.

"Totally," Clarice said.

"Well, your diary says different," Brian added.

Clarice's heart started to beat out of anger and frustration. Had he for real been snooping around her private stuff?

"You little shit," she said wanting to throw her pizza in his face.

"Not that language at the table, Clarice," her father said.

"But, Dad," Clarice said.

"Yell at him with nicer words if you have to."

"That's not possible. I have homework to do. Thanks for dinner," Clarice said and left the table.

She put her plate in the dishwasher and headed back to her room.

Closing the door behind her, Clarice decided to chance out of her red blouse and dark-gray Cavaricci pants into her black silk pajamas and have a chill evening. She did not want to think about her ex; she had done enough thinking about him over the summer. To distract her mind, she walked to the TV and looked through her cabinet of movies. She came across titles like *Kramer vs. Kramer*, *The Outsiders*, and *The Breakfast Club* before deciding on *Friday the 13th*. She then went back to the kitchen and took out a bag of popcorn from the cabinet.

"Are you having popcorn for your second course?" her father asked as he continued to enjoy his pizza.

Clarice did not know what to answer, so instead she said

nothing at all and just walked back to her room as the popcorn was done. She tied her hair up with a scrunchie and got comfortable in her bed full of pillows. Grabbing the TV remote lying on her bedside table, she pressed Play, and the movie started. As she leaned back on her pillows, Clarice started thinking about the day ahead and that it was her time to decide what she and Samantha were going to do.

To be honest, she wanted to go back and see more of Samantha's huge beach house, but it was not like that was going to happen. If Clarice's parents were as rich as Samantha's, she would also want to live on the beach. It looked so peaceful, unlike her own apartment in the middle of town. Not that she was ungrateful. She lived in a beautiful apartment, and her parents had enough money to support the entire family. They were also home almost every evening, unlike Samantha's.

But it sure would be nice to live on the beach.

While filling her mouth with warm and salty popcorn, Clarice looked up toward her ceiling and asked herself, "What would really happen if somebody from school saw Samantha and me out together.

WEDNESDAY

October 15, 1986

The clock showed four minutes past nine as Samantha walked up the stairs in front of the school's main entrance with AC/DC screaming in her headphones. Opening the door, she was greeted by an empty hallway. All the students had already gone to class. It was quiet, and the wind coming from the door caught a few chemistry papers lying abandoned on the floor just by her feet. She threw her big, black leather bag over her shoulder and walked into the girls' bathroom.

Leaning against the wall, dressed in red zebra-printed tight pants and a ripped jeans jacket with studs and KISS patches all over it, Mick whistled as he saw Samantha coming through the door.

"Damn, you look hot," he said and moved toward her to help her with the bag.

Samantha shook her head and dropped the bag on Mick's feet. Luckily for him, it was not very heavy.

"I hope you walked in here after everybody had gone to class," Samantha said.

"How stupid do you think I am?" Mick asked as he picked up the bag from his feet.

"You really want me to answer that question?"

Mick dragged his fingers through his long, dark hair and swung it over his shoulder like he was in some sort of shampoo commercial.

"You brought the Coke bottles, right?" Samantha asked as she walked toward the mirrors on the wall to put some more makeup on.

"They are right by your feet," Mick said.

Samantha took a step back and saw all the Coke bottles, placed under the sink, by her feet.

Going through the bag, Mick laughed as he saw its contents. A red-colored short-haired wig, a 7-Eleven uniform, five bottles of extra-spicy Chinese soy sauce, and a pair of reading glasses.

"This could probably make the Guinness Book of Records for Best High School Prank Ever," Mick said as he threw the white 7-Eleven uniform which landed on Samantha's head. She was busy painting some freckles with a brown eyeliner on her cheeks.

"Would you please spice up the drinks so we can get out of here?" Samantha said, impatient.

Grabbing the five bottles of Chinese soy sauce from the bag, Mick bent down to the Cokes sitting next to Samantha and started to pour the sauce into the half-filled glass bottles.

"It feels like I'm Krankenstein," Mick said as the carbonation started to bubble in the mixture with the soy sauce.

"It's Frankenstein, you idiot," Samantha said while rolling her eyes.

"Well, excuse me, Miss Perfectionist."

Samantha unbuttoned her black, ripped jeans and changed into the white skirt belonging to the uniform before putting on the matching shirt over her Def Leppard top. With his mouth wide open and eyes round like a big circle, Mick stared at Samantha, standing just out of reach in a crop top and hot-red panties. Her legs were shiny from her moisturizing them and they were perfectly toned.

"I would really appreciate it if my death certificate didn't say 'drowned in Mick Thomas Downey's saliva'," Samantha said as she put on the white sneakers from the bag and tied up her hair to get the wig on.

"Oh, come on! You're stripping off right in front of me

and you expect me to cover my eyes?" Mick said.

"No, but I expect you to take those Coke bottles and place them on the trolley, so we can get this over with."

"All right, fine, but you do look great in that 7-Eleven outfit."

"Just do it," Samantha said and put on a pair of shorts underneath her 7-Eleven skirt.

The hallway was still just as quiet as when Samantha had arrived a few minutes ago, but now she was on a mission. She walked with Mick and his trolley behind her, toward the classroom where math was held. She prayed she would not run into any teachers on the way who would sabotage it all.

"Here it is," Mick said and pulled up next to the classroom.

He carefully peeked through the round window of the door and saw that Mrs. Tomson had gone to get her coffee, as always at fifteen minutes past nine.

"It's time," Mick said.

Samantha quickly fixed her red-haired wig before opening the door and entered the classroom alongside the carriage with soy Coke. The classroom was rather silent, besides the two rockers in front who were talking about some hot girl.

"Good morning, students," Samantha said with her best Southern accent.

The students in the classroom looked like individual question marks at seeing the 7-Eleven worker entering their math class.

"It looks like you could use some sugar by this time of the day," she added.

"Hell, yeah," one of the rockers said with laughter.

"At 7-Eleven we have come up with a new idea, to serve high school students all over California soda every Wednesday to keep up spirits," Samantha said behind her big glasses and red-haired bangs that practically covered half of her face. "How does that sound?" she asked while placing a soy Coke on each of the poppers' tables and a normal Coke in front of the rockers.

Everybody in the classroom started to look around to make some sense out of this, but when one of the rockers opened his drink and poured it down his throat, the rest of the class did the same thing.

Within seconds, the classroom turned into one giant soda sprinkler. As soon as the soy mixed with carbonic acid touched the poppers' tongues, they spat it out faster than the blink of an eye, and it covered the desks, floor, and the people in front of the drinkers' hair. It became chaos. People started screaming, giving facial expressions Samantha had never seen before, and two of them opened the window to air wash their tongues from the horrible taste and spiciness. Mick stormed into the classroom after watching the show from the corridor and gave Samantha 'the 7-Eleven employee' a high five.

In the middle of the rockers' little victory dance, Mrs. Tomson came back into the classroom. As she opened the door, she was greeted by a popper vomiting all over her granny shoes.

"What on earth!" she said and raised her hands high up in the air in panic and frustration.

Turing around, she walked straight back out of the room and headed quickly toward the principal's office down the hall. She did not care about knocking—she just walked right in.

"This has gone out of control," she started. "The kids are senseless, and if you don't do anything about it right this second, I will walk out of here and never come back."

"Calm down," Principal Kidman said while looking up from his pile of papers. "Now tell me what happened."

"They destroyed the whole classroom and vomited all over my shoes."

The principal sighed loudly and reached for the microphone that stood by the corner of his desk. He pressed the button and started talking.

"Listen up, fellow students: this is a message from the principal asking all of you including the teachers to stop what you're doing and take a seat in the auditorium. Thank you."

Just as if the fire alarm had gone off, all students got up

from their desks and walked out of the classrooms in large groups.

"Give me my hairspray," Samantha said as she took off the wig in the crowded hallway and let her hair out of the ponytail. She prepared herself to receive the hairspray by reaching out her hand.

Mick opened her bag that he carried on his shoulder and started to dig around as people pushed him from left to right to get to the auditorium.

"I can't find it," he said, sounding like he'd just lost a wallet with a million dollars in it.

"I don't have all day," Samantha said as she took off the 7-Eleven uniform and revealed her Def Leppard top and shorts underneath.

Looking up from the bag, Mick saw a popper in front of him with a hairspray can in his back pocket.

"Here you go," he said after stealing the popper's hairspray and giving it to Samantha.

"Hey, that's mine," the popper said.

Samantha pushed up her hair with her fingers and sprayed all over for about ten seconds before giving it back to the popper.

As the crowd of high school students all walked into the auditorium, Samantha took a seat on the left side, the rockers' side. Up on stage, the principal was talking to Mrs. Tomson and Mr. Morgan while more and more students came into the auditorium. The janitor walked up on stage and handed over a microphone for the principal to talk through.

"Okay, students, listen up," the principal started when everybody had taken a seat. "I know about your differences and that you do not get along very well, and I may have been too kind over the past years."

He looked out over the students sitting in front of him while taking a few extra breaths.

"Back in 1981, I was made aware of the first prank, made by—as you like to call yourself—poppers and rockers," he continued. "And since then, this hobby of yours has just grown and grown. But as your principal, I have responsibility for your safety and your education, and I prefer not to spend my days calling ambulances, the police, construction workers, and plumbers because of your behavior."

Samantha shook her head in slow motion out of enjoyment for Principal Kidman's optimism. A few of the students in the back could not keep themselves from laughing after realizing what this meeting was about. Did the principal really think this would all change because of a talk in the auditorium? Just like he said, this had been going on since 1981.

* * *

"You said there was a call for me," Clarice said as she walked into the principal's assistant's office.

"Yes, your mom is on the phone," Mrs. Richards said. "And she sounded very upset." She continued and walked into the principal's office with some papers to give Clarice privacy.

Clarice grabbed the phone and held it against her ear as her hand started to shake. She waited a few seconds and swallowed a big amount of saliva before she started to talk.

"Mom?" she said with an insecure voice.

"It's me—Samantha."

Clarice's whole body loosened up, and with a loud exhalation, she was back to normal.

"Oh my, that's a relief," she said.

"What do you mean?" Samantha asked.

"I haven't spoken to my mom in over ten years."

"How come?"

Clarice paused for a second to see if Mrs. Richards would be back anytime soon.

"Long story, but why are you calling me here? Aren't you in class?"

"Nah, I went home right before lunch, but it's your day to decide what we're gonna do," Samantha said with Whitesnake playing loudly in the background.

"Oh, that's right," Clarice said. "I need a new pair of jeans from Guess, so maybe we could go to the mall? Or on second thought, maybe that isn't such a great idea."

"I'll pick you up in ten minutes. The rest of the school doesn't end until four, so we'll be safe," Samantha said before hanging up the phone, leaving no time for debate from Clarice.

Putting the phone back on the desk, Clarice left the room with quiet steps before Mrs. Richards made it back to question her about the call from her upset mother.

Since she did not have a proper excuse to leave chemistry class, Clarice did not bother to go back and get her books, still lying open on her desk. She figured Andy would store them in his locker until tomorrow. Instead, she stopped by her own locker to take out her backpack and then continued toward the main entrance. The clock over the door showed 2:05 p.m., which meant that Clarice was leaving school two hours earlier than she should. The fact that she, for some reason, did not care about the consequences of her actions made her feel a bit scared of herself. This was not like her.

Standing by the parking lot, leaning her back against one of the palm trees, Clarice waited for Samantha to arrive. It was just another beautiful sunny day. As she put on her sunglasses, she saw a black Corvette coming from around the corner. From the music being played and the extreme volume, she knew right away that it was Samantha.

"What's that music you're playing?" Clarice asked as

Samantha stopped her car on the sidewalk just in front of Clarice.

"It's KISS," she said and turned the volume up even higher.

Placing her sunglasses on the tip of her nose, Samantha looked at what Clarice was wearing as she took one step closer to the car.

"You want me to pose for you?" Clarice asked as she noticed how Samantha watched her high-waisted shorts and bright pink top.

"Just get in," Samantha said.

* * *

To the tones of "Stuck With You" by Huey Lewis & The News, Samantha and Clarice entered the mall. Clarice smiled when she heard the song play through the speakers of the building. It was way better than what Samantha had just played in the car.

"Oh, come on," Clarice said, looking over at Samantha who danced stupidly to the rhythm of the song.

Seeing the Guess sign lighted up on the second floor, Clarice went straight for the escalator, leaving the dancing Samantha behind.

"Hey, wait up," Samantha said.

Clarice had never seen the mall with this few customers

before. Usually, it was full of teenagers, but then again, Clarice had never been to the mall during school hours.

As they walked into the Guess store, they were greeted by a young man in his early twenties, dressed in Guess jeans—of course—and a black blazer. With teeth white as snow, he smiled at them before asking in what way he could help.

"I need a new pair of jeans," Clarice said.

"Right this way," he said and led them deeper into the store, to a wall covered with all kinds of jeans.

Blue, black, white, stonewashed, ripped, shorts, high-waisted, boot cut—they had it all. The Guess guy started to look through some of the jeans laying on the wide table in front of the covered wall and gave Clarice four pairs to try on.

"I think these could really work for you. The fitting rooms are right over there," he said and pointed at five small rooms being covered with a burgundy red sheet each. "Let me know if you need any help and feel free to try on whatever you'd like."

"Thank you so much," Clarice said.

"Well, I'll just wait right here then," Samantha said as Clarice walked into one of the fitting rooms and closed the curtains.

Samantha started to look and touch the clothes around her and came across a nice-looking jeans jacket, but that was not the only thing. She also came across a student she recognized from school who walked into the store. He looked younger than her. He was probably a sophomore or a junior, but definitely a popper. Just like everybody else of his kind, he was wearing an oversized gray blazer paired with Levi's jeans and sneakers. His hair was curly and golden brown, while his skin was pale as the moon. He headed in Samantha's direction.

"Do not come out," Samantha whispered to the sheet of Clarice's fitting room.

The popper came closer and would spot Samantha at any second. He stopped and looked at two T-shirts, a plain blue one and one with an ocean print on it, before he stood just out of reach of Samantha.

"What did you say?" Clarice said, opening the curtains.

With only her eyes, Samantha informed Clarice about the popper standing right next to her.

"Clarice? Hi," the popper said as he turned around and stood face to face with her.

Samantha turned around to make herself a little less visible.

"Hi, Derek," Clarice said in surprise.

She leaned in to hug him and gave Samantha the expression that now was the time for her to leave if they would want to make it out of this situation safely.

"What's going on?" he asked and looked behind his

back.

"Hello there," Samantha said after being discovered.

Derek looked confused. He was not really sure what he was seeing or what he was supposed to do or how to act. He just looked paralyzed. A popper and a rocker?

"You are Samantha?" he acknowledged.

"I am? Yeah. Maybe you're right."

Derek turned back to Clarice to make some sense out of the situation.

"Were you two here together?"

"Me and her? Are you kidding me?" Samantha said and threw her head back laughing. "I'm just looking for a new jacket. Nice ass though," she added and pointed at the jeans Clarice was wearing.

With a suspicious and unconvinced look, Derek waited for Clarice to say something, but the comment he was waiting for never came.

"Well, I'm gonna leave you two alone, even if you aren't together," he said and stepped out of being in the middle of the two girls.

"See you around," Samantha said and waved as Derek left the store in a rush.

Being alone with each other again, Samantha and Clarice could not help but laugh at what just had happened.

"Did you see his face?" Clarice asked still laughing.

"Oh yeah, I don't blame him," Samantha said. "But now

what do you think about this jacket?"

"It looks kind of nice."

"Great, and so do those jeans, so let's get out of here, because I'm starving."

Once again, Clarice closed the curtains to change back to her own shorts, and Samantha took her jacket and walked up to the payment counter.

Walking out of the store, they both carried a paper bag with the Guess logo on it. The Guess guy thanked them so much for coming and smiled with his teeth, just as when they had arrived.

"I want a milkshake," Samantha said as she looked down at the ground floor where a newly opened milkshake place was located, and it seemed to be really popular according to the long line.

"Works for me," Clarice said and headed back toward the escalator.

The line contained mostly pregnant women and a few young au pairs that actually had permission to visit the mall at this time of day. The café had a nice breeze and looked very all-American, with its white counter, blue walls, and red tables.

"Welcome to Roy's Milkshakes. May I take your order," a young guy wearing a white hat said to Clarice and Samantha.

"I would like a chocolate milkshake with extra

chocolate, please," Clarice said.

"And I'll have the same but with extra, extra chocolate," Samantha added and looked at Clarice like it was a full-on chocolate competition.

Getting their milkshakes, Clarice paid the cashier and thanked him before moving away from the line. They quickly occupied two free chairs by the end on the counter where they had a perfect view of the process of milkshake making.

"Are you going to the game tonight?" Clarice asked and took a sip of her milkshake.

"Nah, I only watch baseball when Mom gets great seats from one of her Dodgers clients."

"So you're a Dodgers fan?"

"No, I'm just there to spot band members," Samantha answered and cracked a smile while looking down at her milkshake. "But you like the sport, right?"

"I don't mind it, but everyone I know seems to play it," Clarice said.

"So I've noticed. Too bad about what happened with your ex-boyfriend."

"For him maybe," Clarice said and played around with the straw in her milkshake.

From the look on her face, Samantha got the feeling that Clarice did not really want to talk about her ex. She started to wonder why and really wanted to know, but was it too early to ask?

"You don't like talking about him?" she asked and tried to make eye contact.

"Does anyone like to talk about their exes?"

"I don't mind," Samantha said and shredded. "All my boyfriends have been T-B-A-B-H."

Finally, Clarice looked up from her milkshake, and she looked confused.

"T-B-what?" she asked.

"T-B-A-B-H, terribly bad at being humans."

"Oh, that's interesting," Clarice said and laughed quietly. "Well, Brad was not a terrible human—until he just left."

"What do you mean? He just left?"

Clarice replied by nodding her head.

"As you know, he got an offer to play for the Houston Astros, and he just left without saying good-bye," Clarice said. "My brother found out about it when it was announced on TV."

"I thought you two broke up because of his knee injury," Samantha said.

"No, but that was the last time I spoke to him. And now he's apparently back and is coaching the high school team."

For a moment, they were both silent while finishing their milkshakes.

"And what's that with your mom about?" Samantha asked.

"She also left. I was around five."

"Do you know why?"

Clarice shrugged.

"My dad said she wanted to find herself. And apparently, I wasn't a part of that."

"You miss her?" Samantha asked.

"Nah, not really. My stepmother Jessica has been a part of our family since I was seven, so she is more of a mother to me than my biological mom will ever be."

Samantha looked at the big clock hanging on the wall over the milkshake machine and confirmed the time with the watch Clarice was wearing on her arm.

"School should be over any minute now. Wanna get out of here?" Samantha asked.

"For security reasons, maybe we should," Clarice answered and got up from her chair. "Imagine the hysteria in school tomorrow if somebody saw us now."

Leaving their glasses on the counter, they walked through the line, still full of pregnant ladies and housewives, and left the café. The mall was still calm and played radio hits like when they'd arrived, but now they played "Panama" by Van Halen, which, of course, Samantha preferred. It seemed to put her in a jolly mood.

"I love this song *sooo much*," she said as they headed toward the exit.

It was hard for Clarice not to smile at seeing Samantha

happy. It was something rarely witnessed. To Clarice, it was like the bad guy in a movie going good in the end. If Samantha had smiled a bit more in school, then maybe she would not be as intimidating as everybody thought.

"I have an idea," Clarice said, coming out of the building.

"What?"

"I get to drive your car," she suggested, her eyes sparking and excitement coursing all through her body.

Samantha stopped for a second on their way to the Corvette and looked at Clarice with a frown.

"Are you serious?" Samantha asked.

"Come on, I'm an excellent driver," Clarice said, sounding very convincing.

"Do you even have a license?"

Digging in her back pocket, Clarice took out her driver's license and gave it to Samantha. Samantha held it in front of her eyes and looked a bit skeptical.

"Um, I don't know," Samantha said. "I love my car."

"I promise I'll be careful, and it might be good for you to take some risks."

Samantha raised her eyebrows as Clarice's comment made her even more unsure.

"Okay then, but if anything happens to it, it's on you," Samantha said and handed over the keys to Clarice who accepted them and opened the car door.

Samantha placed herself in the passenger seat, where she had never before sat, and watched as Clarice turned the keys and slowly backed the car out of the parking space. So far so good, Samantha thought, but she could not relax for a second.

Driving off the main road, it occurred to Samantha that she had no idea where Clarice was going. She drove onto a street full of new-development apartments on each side and small little shops and cafés here and there. All the bricks and red flowers on the balconies reminded Samantha of Paris. The only thing missing was a man dressed in a black beret, blue-striped shirt, and a red scarf around his neck, playing the accordion.

"Are you gonna look for an apartment?" Samantha asked as Clarice stopped the car alongside the sidewalk next to a yellow sign saying, *For Sale*, in big red letters. "'Cause if you are, I think you've found yourself a pretty good neighborhood."

"No, I live in that building over there," Clarice said and pointed at the north building on the right side of the street. "And I thought we could end the day on a good note."

Samantha looked confused at first, but as she watched Clarice get out of her car, she got the point. Clarice had had enough fun for one day.

"Okay then, see you tomorrow," Samantha said.

"See you," Clarice said, as she gave Samantha her keys

back.

Samantha walked around the car, over to the driver's seat, and started the engine. She watched as Clarice threw her bag over her shoulder and walked toward the building she had pointed out. Maybe it was a good thing, leaving it on a good note. Samantha almost wanted to call out Clarice's name and just chill on the beach or something. But instead, she put some pressure on the gas pedal and drove north.

* * *

Samantha walked up to her door and noticed that it was not locked. Had she forgotten to lock it? The thought of an ongoing robbery also crossed her mind. She carefully opened the door and sneaked into the hallway.

"Hello?" she said in the hope of an oral response instead of a physical one.

"Hi, hon," a female voice said from the kitchen.

It was her mother, Linda, the L.A. lawyer who was not supposed to be home until Friday.

"What are you doing here?" Samantha asked and walked down to the kitchen.

"I finished a case and thought I would take the rest of the week off to come home and be with my little family," she said. "Speaking about that case, I just remembered that I have something for you."

Samantha watched her mother, dressed in a dark purple suit, as she walked up to the hallway and started to dig in one of her Chanel bags. What could she possibly have for Samantha?

"Here you go," her mother said as she handed Samantha a paper with the Superior Court of California's logo in the top right corner.

"What is this?" she asked as she looked at the paper. "Am I going to court or what?"

"Turn it over."

She looked at the other side of the paper, and Samantha's heart stopped for a moment. Was this for real? *Thanks for being an awesome fan of our band Samantha, big love Fred Ricky* was written in ink, and Samantha knew for sure it was *his* writing because of all the autographs in her magazines.

"How did you get this?" Samantha asked with her eyes stuck on the paper.

"I was helping him with a case, and I knew you were a fan of his band, so I just asked for an autograph."

"Are you Fred Ricky's lawyer?" Samantha asked in shock. Fred Ricky was the guitarist for the band Eye Candy.

"Yes, I am."

Samantha could not believe it. All along, her own mother had had contact with the hottest guitarist on Sunset Strip.

"So you are the one helping him getting custody of his daughter?"

"That's right," She said. "And from this day on, he has the right to see her three times a week."

"Wow, that's more than you see me," Samantha said sarcastically and looked back down at the autograph written on the paper in her hands.

"He also put you on the list to their show at The Whisky tomorrow," her mother said while laughing. "He must have thought you were at an age to drink and not still in school, so I told him you couldn't come."

"So you did, huh?" Samantha said. "I'm staying over at Karen's anyways." She walked toward the stairs, up to her room.

"I'll call you when dinner is ready," Linda said.

As Samantha entered her room, she immediately threw herself on the bed and took out her diary from under the mattress. With a pen, she started to write.

October 15, '86

Hola, Diary!

It's been a while but I have awesome news. Fred Ricky invited me to Eye Candy's concert tomorrow at The Whisky, and I'm sooo going!!! I just told Mom I'm staying over at Karen's. She seemed to buy it.

In other news, Clarice is not as bad as I thought. She's

actually kinda cool except for her taste in music.

Well, that's all for now. For the rest of the night you'll find me in front of MTV instead of with my history book studying the civil war that took place like 1,000 years ago. Totally not relevant to 1986.

Bye.

THURSDAY

October 16, 1986

The first class of the day was completed, and Clarice walked out of the biology classroom and headed to her locker.

"What were you doing with Samantha, the girl who stood by Hades' side as he decorated the underworld?" Amanda asked as she grabbed Clarice's shoulder from behind.

Clarice wanted nothing more than to tell the truth about Samantha and her being forced together to not be suspended, but it was just too big of a risk. Sure, Amanda was her best friend since freshman year, and they talked about everything with each other, but Amanda was a gossiper. Keeping her mouth shut seemed impossible, and even though she might understand and sympathize with Clarice, she would still tell someone who might not be as understanding.

"I haven't done anything with Samantha, except sabotaging a few of her parties and changing some of her grades," Clarice said.

"Well, you know Derek who lives in the same building as me? He said he saw you two at the mall."

"She was at the Guess store the same time as me. What was I supposed to do?" Clarice said and opened her locker.

"Another love letter?" Amanda asked as she pointed at the piece of paper falling to the ground from Clarice's locker.

Bending down, Clarice picked up the note and looked at it quickly before she added it to her collection of papers in her locker. It said, *I'll pick you up at 8:30,* and she knew it was from Samantha.

"Those adorable little freshmen," Clarice said in an attempt to mislead Amanda.

Without further information, Clarice looked Amanda in the eyes and smiled before leaving for history class. She was one of the first to arrive, except for two quiet rockers sitting in the back of the classroom who never were much harm to anyone. Clarice said hello to her teacher, Mr. Davidson, before she sat down at her desk next to the window. She looked out on the boys and girls laughing in the parking lot, and slowly, her mind flew away on clouds.

At this point, she was not in Long Beach High's history classroom anymore. Now she was lying on a beach, by herself in sunny Hawaii with a *Vogue* magazine and a cold piña colada in her left hand. The wind was soft and gently stroked her tanned skin while the sound of incoming waves from the sea made her whole body feel like it was a part of nature itself.

The door slammed loudly, and Clarice came crashing back to reality. It was Samantha and two other guys being late for class, and they were not the kind of people who were sorry and sneaked in on tippy-toes. Clarice watched as the two guys sat down next to each other and started to drum on their desks and Samantha took the only free seat left in the room, the one next to Mick.

"Hey there, hot stuff," he said as he placed his arm around Samantha.

Pushing him away, Samantha got up from her desk and walked out of the classroom just one minute after arriving. You could hear a pin drop because of the silence in the room, and all eyes were on Mick.

"What?" he asked. "She's hot."

"Downey, principal's office," Mr. Davidson said with his stern voice as he pointed at Mick. "Now."

"May I go to the bathroom?" Clarice asked while raising her hand high up in the air for Mr. Davidson to notice.

He nodded his head in response, and Clarice walked out of the classroom with a very annoyed Mick in front of her. As he walked left toward the principal's office, Clarice walked right toward the main entrance to see if Samantha's car was still parked under the big palm tree as it usually was or if she again had left school. On her way, she was hit by the smell of smoke coming from the bathroom. It had to be Samantha.

"God, that cigarette really stinks," Clarice said as she walked into the bathroom, covering her nose.

Samantha looked so relaxed, leaning against the sink with the cigarette resting between her fingers.

"Have you tried?" Samantha asked and held out her cigarette in front of Clarice.

"Never, and I never will."

"Good for you," she said and inhaled from the cigarette herself.

Clarice walked over to one of the stalls and sat down on the toilet lid with her legs crossed while Samantha watched her and exhaled more smoke. It was quiet, and the smell of smoke and chemicals from hairspray and perfume made Clarice twist her face like she was eating a sour lemon.

"What are you doing here?" Samantha asked.

"I was kinda bored," Clarice said and blew away some smoke coming her way while shrugging.

"Seriously?"

"Nah, I came to see how you were doing," she said, done playing cool.

"Why would you do that? I'm perfectly fine."

"So he didn't offend you?"

"Who? Mick? Are you kidding me?" Samantha said with her eyes wide open as if she'd heard the most shocking news ever. "I'm too used to it to be offended."

"So why did you leave?"

"He's too annoying, and I could never get through the whole class sitting next to him, so I left."

Clarice smiled and shook her head. The fact that Samantha said she'd left class because the person next to her was annoying didn't sound like a valid reason coming from a seventeen-year-old. Maybe from a five-year-old.

The tension in the room changed when Clarice heard another person entering the bathroom. She carefully closed the door to the stall she was sitting in to keep from being seen with Samantha. Through the crack in the door, she saw how Samantha looked down. Whoever had entered the bathroom had to be shorter than Samantha. Maybe it was a freshman.

"And what are you looking at?" Samantha said after exhaling the last breath of smoke from the cigarette.

Without a word, the visitor rushed out of the bathroom.

Clarice had almost forgotten how Samantha approached people, and she felt sorry for the poor little girl who probably just wanted to use the bathroom. That was Clarice just three days ago, and somehow she had ended up here, in the bathroom again, talking to Samantha voluntarily. Samantha was not really a bad person, so why was she so mean? What was she hiding?

"You can come out now," Samantha said, looking at the door Clarice was hiding behind.

"Don't you think that was a bit harsh?" Clarice asked after opening the door.

"If they can't even go to the toilet because I'm standing here, then how are they gonna achieve anything good in life?"

What Samantha said sounded smart, but it made no sense at all to Clarice.

"You can't possibly mean that you act like a total bitch to make the other students tougher and succeed in life."

Samantha raised her eyebrows, shocked that Clarice had just called her a bitch.

"Being kind isn't always the answer," she replied and threw her cigarette out the window after drowning it in tap water.

"Whatever you say," Clarice said and shrugged as she got up from the toilet seat. "I think I need to get back to class now." She walked to the door.

"Fine," Samantha said and watched as Clarice walked out of the bathroom.

When Clarice returned to the classroom, it was as if nothing had happened. The two rocker boys in the back still played every drum solo from Metallica's *Master of Puppets* album on their desks, three rocker girls sat in front of them, trying to untangle each other's headphone wires. Mick was back from the principal's office and sat, once again, in the front by the door half asleep with his big head resting against the wall. Tom and Andy drew something together on paper, and Tiffany, who sat next to Clarice's desk, chewed a large amount of bubblegum, filling the whole classroom with the smell of mint. The rest of the class was either looking up at the ceiling or out the window or were playing with their pencils while Mr. Davidson stood with his back to the students and drew something that was supposed to look like a map of America.

"Why not pull down the photographic map right above?" Clarice thought as she sneaked back to her seat next to Mint Tiffany.

Just as she sat down, Andy handed her the paper that he and Tom had drawn on. It was an invitation to a party at Tom's place next weekend. Tiffany grinned with all her teeth showing and clapped her hands without making any sounds. Clarice accepted the invitation by showing the boys a thumbs-up. They both smiled at her before giving Mr. Davidson their attention.

Clarice could not help but look at the door as she waited

for Samantha to return. But she never came back.

* * *

According to the digital clock on Clarice's bedside table, the time was four minutes to eight thirty. Full from the family dinner, she patted her stomach before going through her wardrobe to find something appropriate to wear for tonight. Clarice had no idea what Samantha had planned, which made it harder for her to decide. She played it safe and put on her white, floral-printed pants and a purple, loose-fitted crop top. Her hair had, after a long day at school, started to fall out of styling. To fix it, she grabbed her black hairbrush and quickly brushed it through before she teased her bangs and sprayed it with a quarter of a hairspray can. She did not do much to her makeup besides improving the color of her warm pink blush and putting on some mascara. To finish off the look, she sprayed a bit of Chanel perfume on her neck and wrists.

"Done," she thought, standing in front of the mirror before going out on the balcony for some fresh air. And she wanted to see when Samantha would arrive.

Just as the clock changed over to eight thirty pm, Samantha's Corvette stood parked outside Clarice's apartment. Who knew Samantha was the type of person who would be on time?

"I'm going out," Clarice said while putting on her jeans

jacket and KEDS sneakers in the hallway.

"And may I ask where you are going?" her father asked as he looked up from the paper he was reading with his glasses on in the kitchen.

"I'm just meeting up with a friend. I'll be back soon," she said, before closing the door behind her and rushed down the stairs.

Samantha rested her forehead against the steering wheel as Clarice walked over to the car.

"Where are we going?" Clarice asked as she sat down in the passenger seat.

"I can tell you that you'll never get in if you're dressed like that," Samantha said and reached back to the backseat where she grabbed a plastic bag.

She threw it on Clarice's lap and started the car engine. Clarice looked confused while opening the plastic bag.

"I guess we are the same size, so put that on," Samantha said.

The bag contained a Whitesnake top that Samantha had cut the lower half off, a leather skirt, black fishnet tights, and a pair of burgundy high heels.

"You've got to be joking," Clarice said.

"Excuse me, but who sacrificed herself and dressed in a disgusting bright yellow bodysuit this week? Oh yeah, that's right, me," Samantha said. "Now it's your turn."

On that note, Clarice, alongside her morals, knew she

had no other choice but to put the groupie clothes on. As they hit the freeway, Clarice undressed, and Samantha did not seem to care that there was a half-naked popper in her passenger seat.

"Happy now?" Clarice asked after transforming from an angel to some devil-looking kind of skank.

"Almost," Samantha said and lifted her butt up slightly to reach the black eyeliner in her back pocket. "This will do the work."

Clarice looked at the eyeliner Samantha held in front of her and sighed. She pulled down the sun shield and got closer to the mirror to carefully draw on the black around her eyes.

"Okay, do you have a tattoo machine around here as well or what?" Clarice asked with sarcasm.

"If I did, don't you think I would have a tattoo on my body?"

"Who says you don't?" Clarice said.

Samantha looked over at Clarice and snorted.

"You look perfect," Samantha said.

"Can you tell me now where we're going?"

Samantha rolled her eyes at Clarice and put on the tape recorder that started to play Ratt.

"Fine," she said. "We're going to L.A."

"L.A.!" Clarice screamed and almost jumped out of her seat. "L.A. as in Los freaking Angeles? What business do you, or we, possibly have there?"

"Calm down. We're only going to a concert on the Strip."

Clarice almost felt as if a lock had been put around her lungs and now she had a hard time breathing. Leaving her apartment, she'd thought they would go to a café or something, but going to a rock concert on Sunset Boulevard had not even crossed her mind.

"You do know they have age limits on those clubs, right?" Clarice said.

"Of course, I know that. I'm not stupid."

"I wouldn't be so convinced about that."

Samantha laid some extra power on the gas pedal as she switched lanes on the freeway. It got darker by the minute, and the street lights lit up the way.

"We're on the list, so no one will ask for our IDs," Samantha said with confidence. "Fred Ricky himself invited us."

"Fred Ricky who?" Clarice asked with a questioning look on her face.

"The guitarist from Eye Candy. Don't tell me you haven't heard of Eye Candy."

"Why would I?"

"Their single "Touch the Night" is on MTV like all the time," Samantha said and raised her hands to show how serious she was.

"Is that the one with the stripper in a red Ferrari?"

"She's not a stripper. She's a dancer," Samantha corrected.

"Whatever," Clarice said and looked out the window. "But my dad is gonna freak."

Samantha drove so fast that the street lights looked like one big line of lights up in the sky.

"He loves you, so he'll forgive you," Samantha said. "The drummer is so hot that not even you would want to miss this."

"Hotter than David?" Clarice asked in surprise.

"Nobody is hotter than David Lee Roth, but if anybody is close, it's definitely Mike Perry."

Clarice looked back out the window and prayed to God this night would end peacefully. Samantha, on the other hand, had a hard time sitting still, and focusing on her driving was not a priority. This night could not go wrong. It was impossible.

* * *

After getting into the club, without any trouble, Clarice watched as the space got fuller and fuller by the minute, closing up on Eye Candy's performance at 11pm. Samantha took a few shots with some older girls—probably in their mid-twenties—at a table next to a group of guys who looked very interested in the girls' upper bodies. But who could blame them? All of the girls were dressed the same, in loose-fitting Daisy Dukes, black bras with studs, leather jackets, and boots. Clarice only managed two shots before she became too overwhelmed by the crowd and the heat that she decided to go out for some fresh air.

Sunset Strip was, for sure, the hottest place to be for some people, but not for Clarice. Outside, the line went all the way up the street, and while singing their throats out to Eye Candy's greatest hits, they also got drunk on cheap 7-Eleven beer. Clarice watched as motorcycles drove up and down the boulevard while she took a few breaths of puke- and emission-tasting air.

"Come on! Eye Candy is starting any second now!" Samantha screamed from inside the club.

Clarice sighed and walked back into the crowded club. The lights were all up, and the instruments stood ready on stage. Samantha grabbed Clarice's arm and dragged her through the crowd that already stood in front of the stage. Just as they got to the fence, the spotlights went off. The Whisky a Go Go was dark as the night itself before the crowd started cheering and the sound of an electric guitar came out of the giant speakers. It was Fred Ricky.

Standing on the left side of the stage, surrounded by smoke from the smoke machine, he was dressed in a black blazer—probably five sizes too big—and a shiny silver necklace. His ashy blond hair was teased, long, and curly. It went all the way down to his nipples that from time to time said hello through his loose-fitted gray tank top underneath the blazer. As he continued to play softly on his neon-green guitar, a drum beat was added.

"There he is," Samantha screamed directly into Clarice's ear. "Mike Perry."

As the spotlight lit up the second member of the band—drummer Mike Perry—the girls in the crowd screamed louder than if they were being murdered in a cheesy horror movie. He was real, and he looked even better than on MTV.

"They look exactly the same," Clarice said and pointed at Mike and Fred.

They both had the same hair color, but unlike Fred, Mike did not have bangs, nor as curly hair.

After the slow and beautiful-sounding intro on drums and guitar, Mike hit it extra hard for their first song, which, of course, was "Touch the Night". The volume was so high that even the walls were partying.

Jumping in from the right side of the stage came the singer, Dylan Carlsen, with his long and straight bleached-blond California hair, black leather pants, and a jeans vest showing just enough of his hairless chest. He jumped high up in the air and started to sing the first verse of the song. He moved to the music as if he had ants in his tight pants while he played around with the microphone cord and sang about some girl named Jane.

Samantha sang along to every song. She even knew the words better than Dylan himself. Meanwhile, Clarice stood like a lonely little fish in a stormy sea full of sharks. The music was too loud and metal sounding for her to enjoy. Everybody around her was jumping, dancing, or pushing themselves forward to get closer to the stage, while Clarice just wanted to make herself as small as possible to not be in anybody's way, unlike the girl in front of her who had had her eyes set on Dylan the whole show.

As Dylan finally noticed her eye contact, he got down on his knees and crawled up to her, singing, "Baby, I want you in the dark with me doin' all sorts of things."

Even though that were the correct lyrics of the song, the girl knew it was meant for her. In response, she slowly dragged her already see-through white top off over her head and gave it to Dylan, who held out his hand in front of her. He took a good look at her juicy C-cups and smiled before going over to the pyro machine where he held out the white top and watched as it burned up in flames and smoke.

During Fred's guitar solo, Dylan once again got down on his knees, but this time, he tapped on a security guard's shoulder and whispered something in his ear. The security guard nodded and walked up to the shirtless girl. Digging around in his big pockets, he eventually found what he was looking for and placed a red-colored backstage pass around the girl's neck.

Clarice could not take it anymore, and Samantha would not win the award for Best Company of the Evening. She was too euphoric to even notice that the naked girl in front of them just got a backstage pass.

When a tall, rather large, older guy behind Clarice desperately wanted to get his hands on the naked girl standing before her, Clarice gave in.

"I'll be at the bar," she screamed into Samantha's ear.

Samantha did not even react to Clarice's comment. She was too busy adoring Mike Perry as he beat those drums like his whole life depended on it.

Clarice took a deep breath out of relief after getting out of the crazy jungle packed in front of the stage. She could finally move again and almost felt like dancing, just because she now could. But Clarice did not dance to rock music. Instead, she went over to the bar, just as she said she would.

"Can I give you another shot?" the bartender asked as Clarice sat down and threw her head in the palm of her hands. "It's on the house."

"Whatever," she said without looking up.

He placed two shots in front of her and set them on fire. The sudden heat got Clarice's attention as she was startled, and she sat up in alarm. The small flames from the shots somehow made her feel calm. There was something so beautiful in its nature. Fire. She looked at it, closely, before she blew it out, squeezed some lime juice into the drink, and poured it down her throat, feeling the burn.

"Good stuff, huh?" he said and gave her two more.

Clarice raised her eyebrows and looked at the bartender, who flirted with his sparkly eyes back at her. She felt sick. Not only did she have four shots circling around her inner system, and a rock concert going on behind her, but also now she had a forty-year-old bartender flirting with her as well.

Since she had nowhere else to go, alcohol seemed to be her only way to escape this place. She took the two other shots he had placed next to her elbow resting on the counter and tried her best not to throw up.

* * *

"Okay, everybody, this is our last song for tonight," Dylan said up on stage, holding a bottle of Jack Daniels whiskey while looking out over the crowd.

"Fuck you if you don't know this song. It's called "Run Away"."

Dennis Ronson—the bass player—started the song by playing on his E-string. Later, Fred followed up on his neon-green guitar and then Mike on his drums before Dylan started to sing their latest single and power ballad, "Run Away". The girls standing right by the stage melted like ice cream in the sun as they watched Eye Candy's final performance of the night.

As a farewell, Dylan poured his bottle of Jack over himself before bowing in front of the audience alongside Dennis, Mike, and Fred. After loud applause, screams and bras thrown on stage, the speakers started to play Europe's "The Final Countdown" as the audience made their way back to a table, the bar, or on to another club for a new live band.

"There you are," Samantha said after spotting Clarice at the bar.

Samantha saw how Clarice swerved back and forth on her stool and how her eyes could not maintain focus.

"Clarice, are you drunk?" she asked.

"That's the first time you've said my name," Clarice said and giggled.

"Come on, Sam. Dennis and Fred are out smoking in the back," a girl Clarice had never before seen said. She grabbed Samantha's arm.

"Wanna join?" Samantha asked.

Clarice shook her head and faked a smile, pretending she was just fine.

"I'll be right back. Don't you move," Samantha said and looked Clarice deep into her eyes before she was dragged into the crowd of people heading toward the exit.

Clarice rolled her eyes and looked around the room. She looked at the men dressed in black that took down Eye Candy's instruments up on stage, the group of girls sitting a few chairs away from her by the bar drinking, and the bartender running from left to right serving drinks.

"Hey there, what's your name?" a sleazy man voice whispered in her ear. "I'm Jerry."

Sitting on her stool by the bar, Clarice slowly turned her head around and saw a greasy-haired male who was at least ten years older than her, with a lot of eyeliner around his eyes. He grabbed a handful of her long, shiny hair and held it in front of his nose.

"Your hair smells so lovely," he said.

He put his warm and sweaty hands on her waist and started to kiss her neck.

The amount of alcohol in her body made her reactions slow and indecisive, but as the bristles from his beard touched her neck, it tickled, and she felt the vodka coming up and down her throat. She took a breath to keep herself from throwing up.

"Please stop," Clarice said and rolled back her shoulder to get him away from her.

"What do you mean? Don't you like it?" Jerry said as he moved his hands from her waist around to her stomach and hugged her tight from behind.

She felt his heavy breathing close to her ear and how his warm, wet tongue made contact with her earlobe. In circular motions, his hands touched her naked stomach and continued down her leather skirt.

"Please go away," she said, sounding like a little girl

about to fall asleep, as she tried to get off her stool.

She lost her balance and almost fell, but he held her tight.

"Oh, you wanna dance?" he said and started to move her hips from left to right alongside his body.

"I'm serious. Let me go," she said and tried her best to get his strong arms off her.

"Hey man, chill out," the bartender said as he came back to Clarice's side after talking to the girls on the other side of the bar. "Don't make me call security."

"Can't you hear what she's saying?" another guy who'd just ordered a drink said. "Let her go." He sounded really serious.

His tall body made him appear more powerful than Jerry, and the determined look in his eyes even made Clarice feel a bit scared. He looked good, though—early twenties, sparkly eyes, and long, teased hair like everybody else's, wearing jeans and a black tank top.

"And what the fuck are you gonna do about it?" Jerry said aggressively and took an even tighter grip around Clarice.

Getting his ordered drink from the bartender, the guy took a good look at it, and instead of drinking it, he threw it in Jerry's face. With looks to kill, Jerry dried his face on his shoulder and blinked hectically to wash away the burning alcohol in his eyes. To prove that he was the boss, he grabbed

Clarice and lifted her up.

"Let me go," Clarice said as she kicked her legs in the air, but her comment only seemed to trigger him even more.

At this point, the other guy had had enough. Jerry had left him with no other choice but to solve this with violence. He tightened his fist, looked Jerry in his drunken red eyes, and hit him right in the face.

"What the fuck!" Jerry said after finally letting go of Clarice and covering his bleeding nose.

Clarice jumped up on the counter to keep her distance from Jerry, who cursed over and over while trying to stop the bleeding from his nose with his hand.

"Now I suggest you get the hell out of here and don't bother coming back," the guy said and pointed toward the exit.

Clarice looked at the two guys in front of her who had created a major scene. With fire in their eyes, they just looked at each other before a security guard grabbed Jerry's arm and walked him out of the club. Clarice's head dropped with relief, and she started to breathe again.

"Can I help you get down?" the guy asked and held out his hand for Clarice to take.

She laid her hand in his, jumped down from the counter, and placed herself back on the chair she'd previously sat on.

"Thanks for what you did," Clarice said and looked down at the floor.

"No problem," he said and sat down on the stool next to her. "But you owe me a drink." He gave a little laugh to show he was kidding.

Clarice giggled and looked up at his face.

"I think I can get that for you," she said and waved at the bartender.

He got her signal and started to mix together another drink of what the guy had previously ordered, and one extra for Clarice, of course.

"I'm sorry if I'm being rude, but you look so familiar," Clarice said with laughter and once again looked closely at his face.

"If you've been here for more than fifteen minutes, then maybe you saw me on stage. My name is Mike," he said and held out his hand again, but this time for a handshake.

Clarice almost choked on her drink. It was Mike Perry, the drummer. Was this real? Or was she too drunk to know if she was dreaming or not? According to Samantha, Mike was the hottest guy in the business, next to David Lee Roth, of course. And he sure looked good.

"So that's why so many people are staring at us—it's 'cause you're famous?" Clarice said and once again giggled.

"Nah, I don't know," he said and almost blushed as he took a sip of his drink. "What's your name?"

"Clarice," she said. "Are you related to that "Living-on-a-Prayer" guy, whatever his name is?"

"You mean Jon Bon Jovi?" Mike asked with laughter.

"Yeah, that's his name. You look very alike."

Mike looked at Clarice in fascination before shaking his head to answer her question.

"Hi, Mike, can we get your autograph?" two girls dressed in shorts and bikini tops said behind them.

"Sure," he said, after turning around. "Where should I sign?"

"Right here," one of the girls said and pointed at the area of her upper boob that was not covered by the bikini.

Mike took the pen that the girl held out in front of him and leaned in closer to sign his autograph on their breasts.

"Thanks," the girls said and grabbed his hair by the back of his head and leaned in to kiss him. He slowly shook his head with a smile as he watched the girls walk away.

"Charming," Clarice said and took another sip of her drink.

"Don't you think you've had enough to drink by now?" Mike asked, as Clarice almost fell off her stool, again.

"Maybe," she said and threw her hair over her shoulder after Mike had stabilized her.

Without asking, Mike took the initiative of taking the drink away from her and poured what was left of it down his own throat instead.

"Hey, that was mine," she said, as she watched him swallow.

He only smiled a gorgeous, wide, white smile.

"Are you here alone?" he asked.

"It depends on how you look at it," she said philosophically. "I came here with another person, but she dumped me for your friends, and now you are here so logically I'm not alone."

"But where do you live?"

"I live in Long Beach," she said and turned around to see if Samantha was back yet.

Clarice looked at the watch around her arm and saw that it was just a few minutes before midnight. Her parents would definitely kill her, if she even made it home in one piece. Where could Samantha be? Had she left Clarice drunk and all alone in Hollywood with only a rock star to take care of her? She started to feel the weight on her shoulders and how her head started to spin. Her eyelids got all heavy, and she decided to rest her head in the palm of her hand on the bar.

Before she knew it, she'd passed out.

October 17, 1986

With her heart in her throat, Samantha ran up the carpet-covered stairs of the hotel. It was three in the morning, but she was more awake than she had ever been before. As she entered the fifth floor, she was greeted with an entire hallway filled with beer cans, whiskey bottles, underwear, and a few empty bags that looked as if they had once held cocaine. She knocked on the door to room number 511 and tried to reduce her heavy breathing by taking one big, deep breath.

After what felt like hours, the door was opened by a naked girl with long, ginger-colored hair and a little diamond nose piercing.

"Is Mike here?" Samantha asked, trying to keep her eyes

on the girl's face.

"Mike who?"

"Mike Perry. This is his room."

It was obvious that the girl was high. She could barely stand on her own legs and had to hold onto the door to keep herself from falling. For every second that went by, Samantha started to feel more and more guilty for leaving Clarice all alone by the bar, all alone in Los Angeles.

"He's in 514, I think," she said as she looked wonderingly at the light bulb in the ceiling.

Samantha faked a smile and helped the girl close the door before knocking on room 514. This time, it was Mike who opened the door. He stood in only his black Calvin Klein underwear and tried to adapt his eyes to the bright light from the hallway.

"What do you want?" he asked with his raspy morning voice while rubbing his beautiful steel-gray eyes.

Samantha just stood there, looking at his shirtless upper body without getting a single word out of her mouth.

"Eh, I'm looking for Clarice," she finally got out. "Do you know where she is?"

With his thumb, Mike pointed toward the bed in his dark room with his clothes laying all over the floor.

Without being invited, Samantha stepped into the room and walked up to the left side of the bed were Clarice was sleeping fully dressed in the clothes Samantha had given her earlier.

"Clarice, wake up," Samantha said and slapped her gently in the face.

"I don't wanna go to school," Clarice mumbled and changed sleeping position.

"Fine by me, but if you don't want your parents to kill you, then you should probably go home and sleep in your own bed."

"What do you mean? Who are you?" Clarice asked when her eyes started to clear.

"It's me, Samantha, and you are right now in Mike Perry's bed," Samantha said and looked for Clarice's shoes that had to be around somewhere in this dark room.

"Okay, just give me a sec."

Samantha gave her the shoes and decided to wait outside until Clarice was ready to leave.

"God, you're so hot," she said to Mike, who got back in his bed and covered his lower body with the white duvet.

He raised his eyebrows and waved her good-bye as she left the room.

"How are you feeling?" he asked Clarice as she scraped off some mascara under her eyes while looking in the mirror over by the TV.

"Did we do it?" she asked.

"You mean, have sex?" he said and sat up in the bed. "No, we didn't, but we did some other fun stuff."

Clarice rolled her eyes and sighed at the overly handsome rocker in the bed who smiled like a sneaky little five-year-old. Her head was still spinning as she remembered scenes from the previous night, although she couldn't remember how she ended up in Mike Perry's room or what 'other fun stuff' he was talking about.

"I must say you are very good at beer bowling, and apparently you're not that into romantic comedies," he added and followed her with his eyes as she walked toward the door.

"Well, they are kinda predictable and never happen in real life, so…," she said and grabbed the door handle.

"You're really leaving?" he asked.

"Yeah, and even if I don't really remember, I'm sure it was nice meeting you."

"But hey, I didn't get your number," he said and sat up on the side of the bed.

"You're a rock star. If you want to find me, I bet you can," she said and closed the door to room 514 behind her and walked up to Samantha who leaned her back against the hallway wall.

Samantha grinned at Clarice.

"You seriously did it with Mike Perry? You of all people," Samantha said. "Do you understand how lucky you are?" They started walking down the party hallway.

"I didn't do anything," Clarice said.

"I don't believe that for a second," Samantha said with a laugh.

Clarice wanted to say something in her defense, but she didn't bother. Her head ached too badly to even walk properly, and talking just made it worse.

Outside the hotel, Samantha's car was parked, and it looked extra shiny and fancy in the moonlight.

"Are you sure you can drive?" Clarice asked.

"Yeah, I only took one shot, unlike you, and it was like four hours ago. I feel totally sober," she said and opened the car door.

"All right, let's go home then."

* * *

After two and a half hours of sleep, Samantha woke up in her bed, the alarm clock howling painfully in her ears. She rolled over to the other side and closed her eyes once again.

"Good morning, Sammy. It's past seven. Time to get up," her mother said, walking into her room and opening the balcony door to let in some fresh air.

"I'm not getting up," she said.

"Oh, yes, you have school, and I have made breakfast downstairs."

As her mother walked out of the room, Samantha stepped out of her warm and comfortable bed and dragged her feet over to the wardrobe. She decided to wear light-blue jeans, a black tank top, and a green zebra-printed blazer on top. After getting dressed, she went over to the bathroom where she tied up her knotted hair and looked at herself in the mirror. The bags under her eyes looked like two black beetles, and her whole face could probably be on the cover for a 'Sleep-Well-or-Else' campaign. Luckily for her, there existed a magical tool for situations like this. Makeup.

"Sammy, your coffee is getting cold," her mother yelled from the kitchen.

Taking out another hairspray from her stock under the sink, she finished off her hair and left her bathroom that now smelled like a chemical lab. She kissed her David Lee Roth poster good-bye and walked down the stairs to the kitchen.

Her mother had sure made breakfast. On the table, there were eggs, toasted bagels, coffee, orange juice, bacon, and all kinds of bread toppings, like butter, jelly, cheese, ham, and a few vegetables.

"All right, what do you want to talk about?" Samantha asked her mother, who sat at the table, reading the newspaper.

"What do you mean?"

"Come on. You only make this kind of breakfast for me when you want to talk about something. So what have I done?"

Her mother looked up from the paper and took off her

reading glasses.

"Fine. Your father came home around two o'clock last night, and he said you still weren't home at that time."

"But I told you I would be at Karen's house," Samantha said and poured herself a cup of coffee.

"That's odd, because Karen called over here asking for *you*."

Samantha raised her eyebrows and looked down at the bagel laying on a white plate with blue edges in front of her.

"Please don't tell me you went to Mr. Ricky's thing in LA."

"Mr. Ricky, that's a good one," Samantha said laughing. "No, Karen must have called here before she called my car phone. I was out driving when she asked when I would come over."

"But why are you here now if you were staying over at Karen's?"

"Because I woke up in the middle of the night with terrible allergies," Samantha said. "They got a dog a few days ago, and I forgot my medicine."

From the look on her mother's face, it was clear she had given up this battle. It was one thing negotiating a criminal out of a prison sentence, but getting Samantha to talk was on a whole other level. Instead, Linda forced herself to believe her daughter, took a sip of her coffee, put her glasses back on, and continued to read the paper while Samantha enjoyed her breakfast in silence.

* * *

"Clarice, I can't take it anymore," Amanda said, as she stood dressed in only her white underwear, running a hairbrush through her brown, curly hair in the school's gym locker room.

"Take what anymore?" Clarice asked.

"You look like shit, you are never home when I call, and you get messages in your locker from a secret admirer. What is going on, and why don't you talk to me?"

Clarice looked at her friend, who still had shiny drops of water running down her legs from the shower. Her eyes looked sad and a bit scared, like a girl who had lost her mother at the supermarket, but she still had that bit of jealousy resting in the corner.

"First of all, thanks," Clarice said with sarcasm. "Second of all, I don't have a secret admirer, and thirdly, I been focusing on doing my homework at the promenade café."

Amanda became silent. She dug after her clothes in the locker and put her wet legs in her blue jeans, one leg at the time.

"Hey," Clarice said. "What do you say about you and me having dinner tonight at the new restaurant by the pier?"

"You sure you're not fully booked?" Amanda said and

raised her eyebrows while looking at Clarice sitting on the desk, fully dressed, waiting.

"I'm sure I can squeeze you in."

With a discreet little smile, Amanda put her pink sweatshirt on and placed the towel and gym clothes in her bag before she squeezed Clarice's hand before and walked out of the steamy changing room.

The hallway was rather empty since the majority of students had gone for lunch already. Clarice always had a strange feeling in her stomach when she walked down the empty hallway. It was as if she was in school all alone. It was so quiet and still, until someone she had not wished to meet came around the corner from where the lockers were red instead of blue. And that someone was Brad, her ex. Amanda stopped walking. She saw Brad and looked at Clarice whose heart started to beat like she was back in gym class.

"I'll wait for you by the lockers," Amanda said and walked away from the exes.

Clarice panicked a bit as she flashed back to her sophomore year when Brad was a senior at Long Beach High, and they'd started dating. He looked just the same as the last time she saw him, but with slightly longer hair. He was even wearing the same navy blue T-shirt with a tiny, white stain in the left corner like the last time.

"I can't believe you still haven't thrown that shirt away," Clarice said as she was left with Brad, who awkwardly put his hands in the front pockets of his jeans.

"Why would I? It reminds me of you and when we painted your boat," he said and smiled.

"Yeah, too bad we never got the chance to go on that trip."

Brad stopped smiling and changed into his serious face.

"Okay, fine, I know I screwed up, and it's all my fault. I shouldn't have left without saying anything, but I sort of wanted it to be a surprise," he said and shrugged.

Clarice felt how the blood in her veins started to rush and how she wanted to slap Brad in the face.

"A surprise? Are you kidding me?" she said. "You move across the country without saying a single word. What kind of surprise is that?"

"Well, when you say it like that, I guess it doesn't sound very good," Brad said and blew his brown lock of hair away from his face. "But let me make it up to you. How about I take you to the movies tonight."

"Thanks for asking but I'm busy," Clarice said as she looked at the watch on her wrist. "And even though I hate you, I am truly sorry about your injury. I knew it was your dream to play professional ball." She backed away from Brad.

It got really quiet for a while as Clarice slowly walked toward her locker down the hall until Brad spoke up again.

"Hey, Clarice," he said with his smooth voice and turned

around to face her.

"Yeah."

"Thanks, and I really am sorry."

Clarice shook her head and looked down at the floor. She did not even want to look him in the eye. She just wanted to move on and not get stuck in the feelings she'd had during the summer.

"Whatever," she said and turned around.

* * *

As always around twelve o'clock, the cafeteria was filled with hungry high school students who all contributed to the crazy volume of noise in their eating environment.

"Hello, Samantha," Chris said and sat down next to her at the table she shared with Julia and Karen.

"Hi, Chris," Karen said with twinkling hearts in her eyes.

"God, it's really sunny in here, isn't it?" Samantha said while looking at the pouring rain attacking the wall of glass from outside.

Chris sighed and took off his black pilot glasses resting on the tip of his nose. He always wore glasses inside, thinking he was a real rock star by doing so. He also wore ripped jeans and the KISS T-shirt Samantha had bought him back when they were dating.

"So a little bird whispered in my ear this morning that you have moved up to the big league," Chris said.

Samantha took another bite of a shiny red apple and looked at the rockers sitting at the table next to her, reading out loud from the latest issue of *Rolling Stone* magazine.

"Well?" Chris said. "No comments?"

"What are you talking about?" Karen asked while looking back and forth at Samantha and Chris who sat in front of her.

"Apparently Samantha ran all the bases last night," Chris said. "With Dennis Ronson."

Julia almost choked, Karen's chin dropped to the floor, and the rockers next to them shifted their attentions from the *Rolling Stone* article to Samantha.

"Hello, we're waiting," Julia said while trying to get Samantha's attention who were too busy looking at her apple.

"What do you want me to say?" Samantha said. "Mr. Stalker over here seems to have all the answers."

"I'm not a stalker. Jake told me," Chris said in his defense and took a cucumber slice from Karen's plate.

"Whatever you say."

"Are you talking about this Dennis Ronson?" a girl from the other table said and pointed at a picture in the *Rolling Stone* magazine of a twenty-one-year-old guy with rich, chocolate-colored long hair, rosy cheeks, and the most outstanding nut-brown eyes that looked like they could jump right out of the picture at any second.

"No wonder you didn't answer the phone," Karen said.

"Was he as good looking naked?" the girl asked.

Samantha tried to stay calm by breathing and thinking about other things, but she sure was an easy target to annoy.

"You went to the Strip without us?" Julia said, sounding all heartbroken.

"All right, fine, I slept with Dennis, and yes, it was great, and yes, he does look great naked, and yeah, I went to the Strip without you," Samantha said and stood up from her seat with steam practically coming out of her ears. "For further questions please call my agent." And she left the losers without lives behind her.

"Don't bother coming over to my place tonight," Julia shouted after her.

"I won't," Samantha said before she disappeared out of sight.

* * *

Clarice took one last look at her menu while the blonde, surfer-looking waitress stood right by her side, impatiently drumming a black pen against her notebook.

"All right, I'll have a salad with extra dressing," Clarice said and handed over her menu to the waitress and watched as she walked into the kitchen to inform the chef about their order.

"Thanks for inviting us, guys," Tom said and took a sip of his Coke.

"Yeah, this is so much better than watching *Dallas* with the family," Andy said.

"Anytime, boys," Amanda said with a smile.

The newly opened Mexican restaurant named Hot Pieces had the perfect location by Long Beach Pier. It was seven o'clock on a Friday night, and the sun was almost completely gone, leaving the restaurant with only its burning candles on each table as their sources of light. With dark furniture and deep-blue walls, it felt like being up in space.

"Have you applied for college yet, Clarice?" Andy asked. "Journalism, wasn't it?"

"Yeah, no, I think I'll follow your lead and work first, or do some internships," Clarice answered. "My dad knows the editor of *Totally Magazine*, so I'm gonna ask if I can intern there during the summer."

"Sounds great," Andy said. "Well, I have actually decided to attend film school in Hollywood instead of playing ball at SDSU."

"Great, then we can share an apartment while I open up my club," Tom said and threw his arm over Andy's shoulders.

"What about me then?" Amanda asked. "I wanna go to Hollywood too. If you want to be an actress, you have to be there."

Tom looked at her with his fringe covering half of his right eye and smiled.

"All right, but only if you take me as your date when you're nominated for an Oscar."

"Deal," Amanda said and got out her hand to shake it with Tom on the other side of the table.

Clarice took a sip of her soda and smiled at her friends.

"So we are all going to Hollywood?" she said.

"Apparently," Tom said with a mild laugh.

* * *

Sitting on the kitchen floor with her back against the white cabinet, Samantha hugged her legs tight with her chin between her knees and looked at the phone lying beside her. She knew it would ring at any second, and when it did, she did not pick up. After a while, the sound of the ringtone screaming for her attention faded in the back of her head where her dark thoughts continued to war. It was almost nine o'clock, and she had not moved for over two hours. It had just been her and the silence of the empty house, her empty world.

Once again the phone rang, and this time, she picked it up.

"Hello, Samantha? Is that you?" she heard Karen say on

the other side of the line.

Samantha gripped the phone and squeezed it tight with every drop of energy she had left in her body before she threw it into the staircase in front of her. The sound of the phone breaking made her breathe again, but it also made her chin shake, and her eyes could no longer contain the flood of salt water wanting to run free down her cheeks. Even though she did not want to, she had to let the tears go.

With a knock on the door, Samantha looked up from her wet knees and felt how her heart started to beat faster.

"Samantha?" a voice said as the front door carefully opened up.

It was Clarice. Samantha jumped up from the floor and dried her tears away with her black cardigan sleeve. Apparently, she had forgotten to lock the door.

"Wha-what are you doing here?" she asked as she cleared her throat and leaned against the kitchen counter like nothing was wrong.

"Have you been crying?" Clarice asked as she walked closer toward Samantha.

"No, why do you say that?"

"I'm not that stupid. Your eyes are all red and wet, and you have mascara down your chin," Clarice said.

Samantha felt a bit intimidated for every step Clarice took closer to her.

"I'm asking you again. What are you doing here?"

"We never said what we were going to do today, so I thought I'd just drop by," Clarice said and walked down the two steps to the kitchen where Samantha stood behind the counter. "And, look, I don't know what kind of relationship we have, but if you want to talk, I'm a pretty good listener."

"No, I'm fine. It's just that I hate everybody in my life so much," Samantha said and sat back down on the floor.

Clarice sat down on the stair where a broken phone and pieces from it laid all around.

"Okay, tell me about it," she said and crossed her fingers around her knees.

"You really want to hear about my problems?" Samantha asked.

"Yeah, I like problems."

Samantha raised her eyebrows and looked at Clarice who sat in front of her, looking all sweet with rosy cheeks.

"Fine. First of all, we have my parents, who'll never leave me alone about my future and their wish for me to be just like them, a doctor or a lawyer. Then we have Karen and Julia, who are the most annoying people on this earth and I can't stand them, and all the guys in school are just horrible. I have nobody."

"But why are you friends with them if you can't stand them?" Clarice asked.

"Because I didn't know any better," she answered and looked up at the ceiling. "Until you and I started to hang out.

And it's not like we are allowed to continue."

Clarice looked surprised at Samantha's comment. Did she just express a feeling of gratitude for someone else than David Lee Roth? And was that 'someone else' for Clarice? She could not get a word out to respond. What do you say to a person you have basically hated for over three years who has just now said her first nice comment to a real person?

"So what did I do differently?"

"For starters, you are probably the first person who has ever wanted to hear about my problems."

"What about your parents?" Clarice asked. "They must ask you?"

"Look around you. Do you see any parents around here?" Samantha said. "No, you don't, 'cause they are never home. They work, eat dinner with colleagues, and spend their weekends on conferences, galas, or like tonight's charity event."

Clarice looked around her and understood more than well that, to live like the Harries family did, you would have to work pretty hard. Just the ocean view was probably worth two years of full-time lawyer's work.

"Wanna try an experiment?" Clarice asked.

"What do you mean 'experiment'?" Samantha asked and did air quotes with her fingers.

"It's Friday night. School doesn't start until Monday. What do you say we just hang out like normal friends for the night and care about the consequences later?"

Samantha tried to prevent herself from smiling, but it did not go so well.

"On one condition," she said.

"What?"

"We order pizza."

Clarice, who just had had a big bowl of salad at the restaurant, was not at all hungry, but she let out a laugh.

"Works for me," she said. "But you better have another phone, 'cause I don't think this one works anymore." She held up a piece of the broken phone Samantha had smashed into the staircase.

"Yeah, let's take the one in my room," Samantha said and laughed.

SATURDAY

October 18, 1986

Clarice opened her eyes, and once again found herself in a different environment. Although this time she did not wake up next to a rock star. No, this time, she woke up on a mattress, surrounded by hundreds of rock stars. Luckily for her, they were all two-dimensional and nailed to the wall. She had no idea what time it was, but the sun shone through the loose white curtains that covered the big windows, and she could hear how the ocean water rolled up on the beach right outside the house.

"Good morning," she said when Samantha opened her eyes and tried to adjust to the sunny room.

Samantha rubbed her eyes and looked at the clock showing 10:34am on her bedside table.

"I think I've had about four hours of sleep for the last two days," Samantha said.

"You're not alone," Clarice pointed out.

Clarice continued to look around the room at the posters on the walls and saw one of Eye Candy.

"Hey, I heard a rumor about you in school yesterday that you slept with Dennis," she said with laughter. "Where did that come from?"

"Apparently a friend of my ex-boyfriend was at the Whisky and must have seen me and Dennis backstage in the bathroom. Now that I think about it, I'm not sure we ever closed the door…"

Clarice stopped looking at Mike's face on the poster and sat up on her mattress instead.

"You mean the rumor is true?" she said in shock. "Why didn't you tell me?"

"And when was I supposed to do that? You slept the whole car ride home."

"You could have woken me up."

"Maybe, but I just didn't think you'd care," Samantha said as she got out of her bed and headed toward the door.

Downstairs, Samantha's parents had made the girls pancakes. The pancakes sat on the kitchen counter, piled on a white plate, covered in syrup. Clarice clearly smelled the sweetness as she walked down the stairs with Samantha in front of her, wearing a black lace nightgown. Outside by the pool, Samantha's mom and dad sat in their dressing gowns, eating bagels with a fried egg and coffee. Samantha saw how her mother read the paper as always and her father exploded with ideas about how to install a Jacuzzi down on the beach.

"Where are you going?" Clarice asked as she watched Samantha head back toward the stairs with the plate of pancakes in her left hand and a carafe of orange juice in her right.

"Upstairs," Samantha said.

"Can't we eat outside with your parents?"

"Are you serious?"

"Yeah, they were so sweet last night," Clarice said, grabbed the door handle, and opened the door out to the terrace.

Samantha's father turned his attention from the ocean as he heard the juice glasses make clinking sounds against the plate of pancakes that Samantha carried out from the kitchen.

"Good morning, girls," he said with a smile.

"Good morning, Dr. and Mrs. Harries," Clarice said and placed the cutlery on the table by the pool.

"Please call me Ed or, at least, Edward," Dr. Harries said.

Clarice smiled back at him while Samantha dragged the parasol from the pool, closer to the table, to hide from the direct sunlight shining on them.

"So how was your thing last night?" Samantha asked,

not even pretending to be interested.

"Thanks for asking," her mom said with an exaggerated smile and took a sip of her morning coffee. "It was actually kind of interesting this time. They talked about expanding the state's medical team to Africa to help with vaccinations and other necessities."

"So are you going to go to Africa?" Clarice asked.

"Oh no, not me," Dr. Harries said. "I'm an cardiovascular surgeon and mostly do greater operations around the West Coast, but a few colleagues of mine are thinking about going away for a month or two."

Clarice took a piece of her pancake and nodded at Dr. Harries's answer.

"So, Clarice, what do your parents do?" Linda asked.

"Mom," Samantha said, as that question always came up when she brought a new friend home.

"My dad runs his own business, an advertising agency, and my stepmother is in charge of Long Beach Bank."

"That sounds nice," Linda said and turned her face toward the sun to better up her tan. "What about your biological mother?"

Samantha took the last gulp of orange juice from her glass and raised from her chair.

"Come on, Clarice. Let's go," she said and gathered her plate and cutlery.

"No, it's okay. I don't mind," Clarice said.

"But I do. Come on."

Clarice ate what was left of the pancake lying on her plate and thanked Samantha's parents for their hospitality.

"No problem," Dr. Harries said and waved as Clarice and Samantha went back inside.

* * *

Clarice's breathing was heavy and irregular after running all up the stairs to her apartment.

"Anybody home?" she asked from the hallway after opening the door with her key.

With no response, she walked into the kitchen and saw a note lying on the dinner table by the window.

Clarice, if you see this it means you are home. We're at the café having lunch and you are welcome to join us, otherwise there are leftovers from last night's dinner in the fridge.

Love, Dad

After eating a late breakfast over at Samantha's house, Clarice could not imagine herself eating more food for at least two more hours. Instead, she walked over to her room and changed out of yesterday's clothes into her black runner pants and a lightweight yellow jacket. As she bent down to put on her shoes, the doorbell rang. It was probably the weekend paperboy who always came late.

"It's open," she shouted from her room.

"Hello?" a deep voice said.

Clarice stopped focusing on tying her shoes and walked out to the hallway to see who was at the door. It was not the paperboy as she first thought. It was Mike Perry, the drummer, casually peeking his head through the front door.

"Going for a run?" he asked as he took his sunglasses off to look at Clarice in natural lighting.

"How did you find me?" she asked in response, kind of shocked since she did not remember giving out her last name.

"Have you forgotten that too? I'm a rock star like you said," he said with a grin. "I have contacts."

Clarice tried to keep herself from smiling at his comment as she more than remembered him being a rock star.

"May I join you?" he asked as Clarice turned off the lights in the hallway.

"Maybe you'd prefer a walk?" Clarice said while laughing as she looked at what Mike was wearing. Skinny black leather pants and an oversized purple blazer maybe were not the ideal running gear to most people.

"It would be more suitable," he said and put his sunglasses back on as Clarice locked the door from outside.

Outside, Mike's sunglasses came to good use as Clarice lead him through the apartment buildings to get to the beach promenade where she would usually run five miles.

"All right, for real," Clarice started, "tell me how you found me."

"Well, you know, I called the Russian mafia and asked them to follow you and get back to me with your address," Mike said.

Clarice stopped for a while and gave Mike a killer look since it was not the answer she wanted.

"Okay, fine, long story short, I asked Fred who invited Samantha, and he said Samantha was a student at Long Beach High, so I called the school and asked for a Clarice. When the woman said they had a Clarice Kennedy, I figured it was you and made up some story about you winning a scholarship, and they gave me your address. Not that fancy."

"So you knew I was still in high school?" Clarice asked, feeling a bit guilty for not telling him.

"You can never be sure, but I had my suspicions."

"How old are you, by the way?" she asked since she had never really thought about it earlier.

"Twenty-one," he said and put his hands in the large pockets of his blazer. "So please tell me you're a senior, so I'm not a total pervert."

Clarice laughed.

"Yeah, I'm a senior," she said and looked out over the ocean.

The beach promenade was quite calm considering it was

a sunny Saturday. Maybe it was because it was lunchtime and the population of Long Beach occupied the cafés and restaurants instead of the promenade, although a few people were swimming in the sea or playing with blown up killer whales, and two teams played a game of volleyball up on the beach.

"Did you know I was a kick-ass volleyball player as a kid?" Mike asked as he stopped to watch a bit of the game going on.

"Why would I know that?" Clarice asked. "I met you for the first time less than forty-eight hours ago."

Mike leaned against the fence and looked at Clarice standing next to him. Her hair danced in the wind coming from the ocean.

"I thought maybe you had read the latest issue of *Rolling Stone* magazine."

Clarice shook her head and put her hair up in a ponytail to get it out of her face.

"To be completely honest with you, I had barely even heard your band before Samantha forced me to go with her to your show," she said.

"Oh," Mike said, a bit embarrassed as he slowly started to walk again. "Well, that makes so much more sense."

"More sense than what?"

"More sense to why you're not begging me to sleep with you," he said laughing.

Once again Clarice stopped, but this time, she did not stop to watch volleyball. This time, she stopped to question Mike.

"I don't even know you," she said.

"Never heard that excuse before," he said, making a face expression, showing his surprise.

Clarice rolled her eyes after remembering who she was talking to. This was not a typical Long Beach High student. This was a drummer in a well-known rock band, and he probably got laid ten times a day.

"Clarice, hi," a female voice shouted in front of her.

After getting a bit closer, she saw that it was Teresa from her math class. Clarice considered turning around and walking straight back home, but she quickly realized that she really had no other choice but to face Teresa with the truth.

"Are you out walking?" Teresa added when she got closer to Clarice.

"Yes, that's exactly what I'm doing," she said and nodded her head.

"And who is this?" Teresa asked and looked up at Mike, who probably was about a whole foot taller than her.

"This is Mike," Clarice said. "He's my cousin visiting from Chicago."

Mike turned his head from looking at Teresa to looking at Clarice while Teresa held out her hand to greet him. In an attempt to not ruin Clarice's plan with his Californian accent, now that he apparently was from Chicago, Mike shook Teresa's hand in silence.

"Unfortunately, we have somewhere to be, but I'll see you around," Clarice said to round off the awkward, little meeting.

"Yeah, I'll put the answers for next week's math test in your locker on Monday," Teresa said as they started to go separate ways.

"So you're a math cheater?" Mike asked when they were once again alone with each other on the promenade.

"Maybe," she said and looked the other way. "I'm not very good at it."

"Interesting. But what the hell was that?"

Clarice exhaled loudly and looked at the incoming waves from the ocean.

"If there is one thing to know about Long Beach, or at least Long Beach High, it is the fact that poppers and rockers don't hang out. And you are more than clearly a rocker," Clarice said.

"All right, you lost me. What's a popper?"

"I'm a popper. I listen to pop music," Clarice said, as she pointed at herself.

"But I'm not even in high school," Mike said.

"Doesn't matter. You still listen to rock music. You even write and play it."

"So because you listen to The Pointer Sisters and Duran

Duran, it means we can't hang out?" he asked.

Clarice for sure heard how stupid it sounded, and it was stupid, but what could she do about it? Those were the rules and if you did not follow the rules you would be thrown out like trash and have no friends.

"But you sure looked like a rocker at The Whisky," Mike said. "Whitesnake shirt and all that."

"Those were Samantha's clothes, not mine."

"Now that's another funny thing. Samantha to me seems to be a rocker, and you hang out with her."

Clarice had had enough. After almost four years of this shit and talking nonstop about it with everybody on planet earth, she could literally burst into one thousand pieces just thinking about how messed up it all was.

"Long story. Can we talk about something else now?"

"Sure, but as a high school graduate myself, I'm gonna tell you a little secret," Mike said. "High school is not your whole life, and you'll barely remember any of your classmates or see them again after you graduate, so live a little and stop caring about them."

"I guess you're right, but still…," Clarice said as she looked up at the sky and repeated Mike's words in her head.

High school is not your whole life. Don't care about them.

* * *

"I have to warn you," Mike said after opening the door into Clarice's apartment building, "parents aren't usually big fans of mine."

"Don't worry. They won't even notice you," Clarice said, walking up the stairs.

"Maybe I should just leave. We could hang some other time."

"Chill out," she said as she opened the door that now was unlocked, meaning her parents were home for lunch, and froze when she saw her brother, standing in the hallway with his curly brown hair disheveled.

"Hey," he said and pointed at Mike. "I saw you in *Rolling Stone*."

"Okay, you're right. Let's not do this now," Clarice said as she turned around, faced Mike and dragged him out of the apartment. "See you some other time."

* * *

Samantha walked over to the phone ringing on her bedroom floor.

"Hello," she said.

"I have a little problem," Clarice said on the other end of the line.

"Okay."

"I might be a tiny bit interested in Mike."

"You mean Mike 'Eye Candy' Perry?" Samantha asked.

"Yeah."

"Oh my God, Clarice, he's a rock star, and you had a one-night stand. Even though I hate to say it, you need to move on," Samantha said. "Those are the rules."

"First of all, I told you we never did anything that night, and second of all, when having a one-night stand, you never see each other again, and I saw Mike just a few minutes ago."

Samantha felt how a wall built up in her throat, blocking every possible word she could think of from coming out. Her heart started to pound, and she had a hard time deciding if she felt jealous, happy, or just confused.

"But I dropped you off just two hours ago," Samantha said.

"I know, and he knocked on my door about five minutes after."

"Okay, Clarice, call him immediately and ask him and some other member of the band to hang out with us tonight."

"That's where my problem comes in," Clarice said. "I have zero of his contact information."

Looking out through the window, Samantha wondered how she could solve this situation. And just like that, she came up with a plan.

"I'll be right back," she said and hung up the phone.

She quietly walked down the stairs and sneaked into her

mother's office. Samantha had never before in her life seen so many piles of papers. They covered the entire desk and the shelves, and on the floor by the window, there was a whole moving box filled. How in the world would she find the paper she was looking for?

She started to look on the desk. Nothing. On the shelves, the binders were organized by month. She took out and opened the binder with the label October 1986 on it and figured that her clients were stored by their surname.

There he was—*R* for Ricky. Fred Ricky. The papers contained all sorts of information, like personal information, information about his ex-girlfriend and their daughter, court dates, judges, and lots of other stuff.

Fred Ricky, born on May 12, 1962, home address 16432 Chapel's Road, Bel Air, phone number 555-832540, work phone 555-643819.

"Jackpot," Samantha thought herself and picked up the phone, hidden under papers on the desk. As she dialed the number, her hand started to sweat. She was really doing to do this, calling Fred Ricky of Eye Candy.

The phone continued to ring, and Samantha lost hope of him answering. But she did not give up. Instead, she called his work phone, although she had no idea where that would take her. Since he was a touring guitarist, he didn't really have an office like a normal person.

"Greg," a deep, dark voice said after two rings.

"Um, hi, my name is Samantha," Samantha said. "Where am I calling?"

"This is Hungry Studios," the man said.

"Perfect, I'm looking for Fred Ricky," Samantha said, sounding confident.

It got quiet for a while, and she wondered if she had said something really stupid.

"He went out a few minutes ago, but Mike and Dylan are here if they can help you in any way."

"Great, I can talk with Mike," Samantha said, her heart jumping on the inside.

"All right, let me get him for you," Greg said and left the phone hanging.

"Mike," Mike said after he cleared his throat.

Samantha recognized that voice more than well. It took her right back to when she'd stepped into his hotel room, and he was dressed in only his underwear. And that raspy morning voice. She got goosebumps just thinking about it.

"Hi, Mike, it's Samantha, Clarice's friend, or whatever."

"The rocker, yeah, I know who you are," Mike said as he let out a little laugh on the other side of the line.

"Good," Samantha said. "Well, I'm calling because Clarice wants to see you again tonight, and to be honest I wouldn't mind tagging along."

"So she does, huh?" Mike said. "Well, we have a deadline for the new album, so unless you want to come to the studio, I'm afraid we'll have to make it another day."

Samantha's heart pounded as she thought of the idea of seeing the members of Eye Candy again. And this time, it would not be from the audience but in person. She sort of knew how Mike and Dennis were offstage, but Dylan and Fred she had only heard rumors about. According to *Tiger Beat* magazine, they were the crazy ones.

"We'll be there," Samantha said.

"Great," Mike said. "It's on the street behind the Troubadour."

* * *

Clarice was hit by the smell of damp and mold as Samantha opened the blue metal door leading into the studio located on a tiny street with only a few containers and black garbage bags as inhabitants. On the other side of the door, there was a short hallway with dirty, white stone walls and red carpet floors. On each side of the wall, there was a door—one leading to a storage room and the other one to Eye Candy's recording studio.

"Should we really do this?" Clarice asked as Samantha placed her hand on the door handle. "I think I'm having second thoughts."

"No time for thinking, the love of your life is on the other side of this door," Samantha said and pushed down the handle.

Entering the room, Samantha and Clarice watched as Fred stood with his guitar and headphones in the booth, trying to nail a guitar solo, while Mike and Dylan sat in one out of two sofas, laughing about something only they knew about, and Dennis leaned over the producer's shoulder, watching every move he made on the big and colorful mixer board.

"Girls," Fred said from inside the recording booth as he was the first one to notice their presence.

"Hey, you made it," Mike said and got up from his sofa when he saw Samantha and Clarice standing in the doorway.

"We sure did," Samantha said and placed herself on the sofa Mike had heated up before her.

Leaning against the wall, Mike scratched himself under his nose and looked down at Clarice, waiting for her to say or do something.

"So, what are you guys doing?" Clarice asked as she kept her eyes on his shoes.

"Well, myself, Dylan and Dennis are mostly chillin' while Fred is trying to get that guitar solo right, and it's now been over half an hour."

"That sounds interesting," Clarice said.

Samantha watched Clarice and Mike as they stood stiff as sticks in the doorway, barely talking to each other while she felt how Dylan moved up closer to her.

"Hello, sweetheart," he said with his raspy voice smelling like breath freshener and Jack Daniels. "What's your name?"

"Hey, Samantha," Dennis said, wanting to join the conversation that was about to happen on the black sofa.

"So you remembered my name, huh?" Samantha said and flirted with her eyes at Dennis, who sat down next to her. "I'll take that as a good review."

Even though she played it cool on the outside, Samantha's heart was beating as if she was seconds away from a heart attack on the inside. She had Dylan Carlsen on her left and Dennis Ronson on her right, and they both were begging for her attention like two needy little kids.

"So, Samantha is your name?" Dylan said and moved up even closer to get a better look down her shirt.

"It sure is," she responded and exhaled a large number of butterflies from her stomach.

"Well, Samantha," Dylan started, as he laid his arm over her shoulders. "Maybe you would like to join me over at the Rainbow when this is all wrapped up."

She tried her best to stay calm, but she could feel how her legs started to shake from the nerves. "Keep your shit together," she silently told herself and looked over at Dennis who fake coughed for her attention.

"I was kinda thinking about going to the Roxy and hanging with Pure Dolls," Samantha said and crossed her legs to hide the shaking, as she looked back at Dylan.

"What the fuck?" Dylan said. "They are so boring you're gonna fall asleep before they even serve you cocaine."

"If you're claiming yourself to be more entertaining, then fine, I'll join you, but you better be worth it."

"Oh, I won't let you down baby," Dylan said with a sleazy smile on his lips.

* * *

About forty minutes later, Fred finally completed his solo for the song, and it was Mike's turn to add some drums. Since he had made himself so comfortable on the sofa next to Clarice, he sighed as he had to get up. Clarice felt as if a part of her was ripped away as Mike moved his big arms away from her shoulders and got up from the sofa. Even though she had only known him for a few hours, the thought of him leaving her made her feel scared. God, he was only going ten steps away to play the drums.

"I know that look, Clarice," Samantha said as she left Dylan and sat next to Clarice. "You have to stop. I'm warning you."

"What look?" Clarice asked as she turned her focus away from Mike to Samantha.

"You're starting to like him, and believe me: I don't blame you. But you have to stop."

Clarice sighed and looked at Samantha's tiny scar on her left temple.

"How did you get that scar?" Clarice asked to change the subject,

"I stabbed myself with a Barbie's arm when I was four, but don't change the subject please," Samantha said.

"Fine, but you were the one who took us here, and if you hadn't I would have been sitting at home in my bed, alone, crushing over some actor on the ABC Saturday night movie."

Samantha wrinkled her forehead.

"I bet even you heard how depressing that sounded, and that's exactly why you are here instead. All I'm asking is that you don't develop feelings for him."

"And why would that be so bad?"

"God, you don't get it, do you?" Samantha said as she rolled her eyes. "These guys aren't like Emilio Estevez in your Brat Pack movies."

Clarice sat up and looked at Samantha, who had never looked more serious, except for when talking about David Lee Roth in the music store.

"I know this may come as a shock to you, but I actually knew that," Clarice said. "But Mike is different."

"Whatever you say, but at least I've warned you," Samantha said and turned her attention to Dennis, who approached her with a big smile and a gaze of temptation.

* * *

After what to Clarice felt like years in the studio, Dylan finally came out of the booth after laying vocals on their current recording and was now ready to leave. The clock had just passed half past ten, and everybody in the room tried their hardest to keep their eyes open. The heat and lack of air in the room made all of them tired, but it did not stop Dylan from wanting to go to the Rainbow and have a party.

"All right now, let's go," he said and grabbed his jacket, laying on the side of the sofa.

Since Dylan invited Samantha, Samantha had to invite Clarice, who, of course, wanted to bring Mike, and Fred and Dennis did not have a good reason why not to join, so instead of going as a duo, they were now six people attending the Rainbow Bar and Grill.

"The bus company asks where they are supposed to pick you up tonight," the producer said who had just answered the ringing phone as he scratched his long, ginger beard.

"What are you talking about now, Ted?" Fred asked as he laid his arm on the producer's shoulders.

"You are leaving for the tour at midnight, and the bus company wants to know where to pick you up."

Everybody paused after hearing the news. Even Clarice and Samantha were surprised.

"Fuck, I forgot to pack," Dennis said.

"I'm gonna fire that manager of ours once and for all," Fred said and kicked his foot into the wall by the door. "Tell them to pick us up at the Rainbow then."

"All right," Ted said and reported the band's answer to the bus company over the phone.

As they left the studio, Clarice watched as Mike got into his car, a red Ferrari.

"Samantha, is that the car from the video on MTV?" she asked and pointed at Mike's car.

"It sure is," Samantha said as she got into her Corvette.

Fred turned on the engine to his new Harley, and Dylan placed himself in the passenger's seat of Dennis's black Porsche since Dylan was under probation for drunk driving two weeks earlier.

On their way over to the club, Mike had his gas pedal pushed down all the way to the bottom while Fred from time to time drove past him on his Harley, begging for a race. With his long and curly hair blowing like crazy in the wind, Fred looked at Mike with a grin and drove past him one more time before arriving at the Sunset Strip. People were lined up outside every bar, and it was not even eleven o'clock yet. But at the Sunset Strip, time was not an issue. As long as the sun had gone down and the alcohol was out, people lined up and partied as hard out on the streets as inside the clubs.

Walking into the Rainbow with Dylan's heavy hand on her hip, Samantha felt as if she had been struck by lightning as the wave of Sunset Strip energy overwhelmed her body, from her head to her toes. The lower floor of the club was filled with red half-moon-shaped sofas and dining tables with colorful pills, cocaine powder, beer cans, whiskey bottles, and a set of ketchup and mustard on each one of them. The people sitting on the sofas were either as alive as they had ever been or as near death as they had ever been, and to be honest, to Samantha it was kind of freaky.

Since the Rainbow was one of the hottest places to be on Sunset Boulevard, it was no surprise that every table was taken. Although for a band with a record contract, that was an easy problem to solve. Walking up to a table, occupied by three guys in their early twenties, Dennis took out a one-hundred-dollar bill from his back pocket and held it in front of the guy who sat the closest. The guy looked at the bill and hesitated for a while before accepting it and got up from the table with his friends.

"Ladies first," Dennis said and invited Clarice and Samantha to take the middle seat of the sofa.

"Hey, give us six beers and a giant plate of French fries, would ya?" Fred said to the middle-aged waiter who just walked past their table, headed toward the bar.

"Will do," he said and left.

Samantha looked over at Clarice who had whispered something in Mike's ear that made him laugh like a little twelve-year-old. It was odd, seeing a popper like Clarice make a member of a rock band laugh the way Mike did. She wondered what they talked about but decided to make her own conversation with the other boys in the band.

"So, how long will you be on tour?" she asked.

"No idea, I didn't even know we were going at all," Fred said and took a sip of his beer that just arrived.

"December, I think," Dennis said.

"So what do you think will happen to those lovebirds over there?" Samantha asked and pointed discreetly at Clarice and Mike who seemed to be on a completely different planet from everybody else under this crazy roof.

"You know the drill," Fred started. "New city, new girls. Little Mickey has ten new ladies on his lap by tomorrow night."

Samantha thought about the idea of not being bound to one single person and having the option to sleep around with whoever without any questions asked. It sounded perfect, but was that something only rock stars were allowed to do? Samantha herself was called a slut just for sleeping with Dennis, although she didn't mind. It was not like any of the people calling her that would accomplish what she had. Losers.

"So you're not a girlfriend kinda band?" Samantha asked in a flirty way.

"When was the last time you had a girlfriend, Dennis?" Fred asked and laid his arm over Dennis's shoulders.

"Probably senior year in high school," he answered with a mild laugh. "But Mike always stole my girls."

"Yeah, he's quite the charmer," Fred said.

"Right, you two went to high school together," Samantha said.

"Not only high school. Kindergarten through junior high as well," Dennis said. "Mike literally lived at my place between the age of twelve and fifteen."

It was really hard for Samantha to imagine Dennis and Mike going down a high school hallway together and even harder to see them playing hide-and-seek in kindergarten, although she thought it was kind of cute that they had been friends for almost their entire lives.

"How come?" she asked.

"Mike's parents weren't really parental material, and I lived on the same block," Dennis answered. "So he would come over when it got too out of hand."

Samantha smiled at Dennis before looking over at Dylan out by the corner. Dylan had been overly quiet since their arrival at the table. He was the one who had promised her a good time, and he was not really delivering. She noticed how he was pulling some weird faces while his eyes were closed, and it did not take long for Samantha to figure out what was going on. Peaking under the table, she saw exactly what she had expected. Between his legs, he had a blonde girl dressed in a black bra with studs and a tight leather skirt with fishnet leggings underneath.

"Look," she said to Clarice and navigated with her eyes.

Clarice looked under the table like Samantha asked her to, with a big question mark on her forehead, and did not know whether to laugh or to panic over what she saw. In the end, she went for both, and Mike asked what was going on with her.

"Dylan is getting a blowjob right next to you," she said.

"You have never been here before have you?" Mike asked.

"No, why do you ask?"

"Blowjobs literally come with the beer. And Dylan is quite a fan of the beer."

Clarice faked a smile to hide her panicky feelings from Mike who threw his head back with laughter. To him, this environment was home, and to Clarice, it was like being dumped on a random Star Wars planet.

"I need to use the bathroom," Clarice said.

"All right, can you find it yourself or do you want me to follow you?" Mike asked.

"If I want to make it there alive in this jungle house, I guess you'll have to come with me," she said.

"Very well," he said and took what was left of his beer before kicking Dylan's leg, asking Dylan to move so they could get out of the sofa.

"Just a second," Dylan said and patted the girl's head

under the table as a signal he was satisfied.

To Clarice, walking inside the Rainbow was like being in a game of Pac-Man, stuck in a labyrinth with people trying to eat you alive. Both Clarice and Mike got dragged from left to right, and to prevent being separated during their journey, Mike grabbed Clarice's hand and tried to get her safely to the bathroom. His hand was so big and warm, and despite the environment, Clarice had never felt safer in her entire life.

"Here they are," Mike said and let go of her hand. "The famous Rainbow bathrooms."

Clarice nodded her head and looked at the sign showing the ladies room.

"But I should warn you that it might be kinda wild in there," he said.

"Not much can beat what I have already seen since arriving," Clarice said. "But you wait here just in case." She held up her finger while looking deep into his eyes.

Mike did not even have the time to look the other way before Clarice was out of the bathroom again.

"That went fast," he said and laughed.

"This place is mental," Clarice said and grabbed Mike's arm, preparing for their return to the table.

It was not just the quantity of people, drugs, and alcohol under the same roof that was crazy about The Rainbow. It was how the amount of people, drugs, and alcohol were used at The Rainbow. Clarice could not help but to watch as a group of guys licked white cocaine off of a girl's half-naked body on the table to her right, and how those on her left poured vodka and champagne into each other's mouths, straight from the bottle.

"Are we finally leaving?" Clarice asked with relief as she saw how Fred, Dylan, Dennis and Samantha got up from their table, located closer to the bar.

"Their tour bus is here, and Dennis said they could drop us off in Long Beach on their way to San Diego," Samantha said and smiled out of happiness.

As long as she got home and could sleep in her own bed, Clarice was happy and walked toward the exit after Dylan, who looked for last minute girls to pick up for the trip.

Out on the street, a big, shiny tour bus waited for them in the open moonlight, and a few members of the Eye Candy crew smoked cigarettes out in the fresh air before boarding.

"What do we do with the cars?" Samantha asked.

"Give your address and keys to Tony in the Mets cap over there. He'll fix it," Fred said and jumped on the bus.

Samantha took a look at the line outside the Rainbow and the fans screaming for Dylan as he waved to them before getting on the bus. She gave her keys to Tony and took one last look at the wonderful Sunset Strip scene. She wondered if this was something she would ever live through again, hanging around clubs with rock stars and all.

"Of course you will," she told herself. Maybe Clarice

was her lucky charm in all this. With a smile on her lips, she got on the bus that was ready to leave for new adventures. And, of course, Long Beach.

SUNDAY

October 19, 1986

"I hate him," Clarice said and walked off the bus with heavy, determined steps.

It was around one o'clock in the morning, and the big black tour bus stopped for gas at a station not too far away from Clarice's apartment.

"Clarice, wait," Samantha said and walked after her.

Their hometown was calm and quiet at this time of the day, unlike Sunset Boulevard, which only got crazier by the minute until sunrise. The sky over Long Beach was dark, and the stars were shining bright, just as if somebody had spilled thousands of tiny diamonds all over it. As Samantha got up to speed with Clarice, she laid her hand on Clarice's shoulder and slowed her down.

"It wasn't that bad," Samantha said. "I've heard a lot worse stuff from when he starts drinking."

"Not that bad?" Clarice yelled and turned around to face Samantha. "He screamed at me and tried to rape me."

"I wouldn't really classify Mike asking you to take off your shirt as rape."

Clarice shook her head and continued to walk downhill toward her apartment.

"Whatever. I'm just gonna forget he ever existed," she said.

Samantha wanted to say, "I told you so," but what difference would that make now? What she had feared would happen had obviously just occurred, so no need for Clarice to feel more regret than she probably already did. Maybe she should have told Clarice about Mike's drinking problems, but all she wanted was for Clarice to give her taste in music a chance. And if anybody could turn a popper into liking rock music, that anybody would be a sober Mike Perry.

As they walked down the hill to Clarice's street, Samantha saw a taxi driving toward them. With a sudden movement, she waved at the driver, who pulled over to the side of the street.

"Don't get too caught up with it," Samantha said. "I'll call you," she added and ran across the street to the cab that would take her home.

Clarice watched as the car's headlights disappeared over the hill, leaving her all alone in the dark, with only her thoughts as company. She looked up at her apartment, and could not wait to sleep her thoughts away, in her own bed.

* * *

It still felt like in the middle of the night when Clarice's stepmother, Jessica, knocked softly on her wooden door. As Jessica entered the room, she walked over to the window and pulled up the blinds to let in the sunlight.

"Good morning," she said and placed herself on the side of Clarice's bed with a breakfast tray in her hands.

Clarice did her best to open up her heavy eyelids. She tried to say, "Good morning," back to Jessica, but her dry and raspy morning voice did not want to be a part of it.

"I've made some breakfast for you," Jessica said and tried to find a stable spot on the bed to place the tray.

Clarice gathered her strength and got up into a sitting position while trying to adjust her eyes to the sunlight creeping in through the window. She looked at Jessica, who had her wet, blonde hair up in a hairgrip and her tanned skin covered in a black maxi-dress. She really was beautiful. On the white breakfast tray, there was a champagne glass filled with homemade orange juice, a plate with a croissant and two crispy bacon strips, a bowl of cereal, and a cup of hot, steamy coffee with two tablespoons of milk, just as Jessica always made it.

"May I talk to you about something?" Jessica asked as she looked at her stepdaughter's messy hair.

"Sure, what do you want to talk about?" Clarice asked and took a bite of her croissant.

"You have been coming in late, if even at all, three nights in a row, and neither your father or I know where you have been or what you have been doing," she said and laid her hand on Clarice's leg. "I just want to be sure that you are safe and that at least *you* know what you are doing."

Clarice had been waiting for this conversation to come up since she came home at four o'clock Friday morning. Luckily for her, it was Jessica who brought it up instead of her dad, who would not have been as calm. Clarice did not like to lie, but this time, it was not a case of "I forgot to call" or "Sorry, I fell asleep watching a movie." This time, she had been out on the Sunset Strip, surrounded by rock stars, sex, drugs, and alcohol. Not even Jessica would be able to stay calm with that information.

"I made a new friend in dance class who just moved here from Texas, and her family has not yet installed their phone, so I couldn't call when I spent the night," Clarice said. "I'm really sorry. I'll try to give you more information next time." She bit her lip as she felt horrible about lying.

Jessica wrinkled her nose and looked a bit skeptical after

hearing Clarice's excuse, but she decided to trust her to avoid conflicts and complications. After all, Clarice had always been honest growing up. Jessica leaned over the breakfast tray and gave Clarice a kiss on the head before walking out of the room.

Clarice placed the tray on her bedside table and got up from her bed. She walked over to her closet and changed from her light-blue pajamas into a pair of shorts and a Long Beach High sweatshirt. As she looked at herself in the mirror, she saw her hair was all out of control, so she tied it up with a blue scrunchie to get it out of her way. She grabbed a pen, notepad, and her Walkman from her desk and the champagne glass with orange juice before she opened the balcony door with her foot since both of her hands were full.

The temperature outside was pleasant, not too cold but not too warm either. She put on her headphones and started playing Irene Cara. With a red Santa Claus pen in her hand, she opened a blank page in her notebook and took a deep breath. This was it. It was time to write what had been the purpose of this entire week. Who is Samantha Harries?

Clarice Kennedy
10/19/86
Week 42
My name is Clarice. I am just an ordinary seventeen-year-old girl, but at Long Beach High my last name is

'popper'. Besides learning how to solve equations and about the inciting factors of the Civil War, LBH taught me how to look down on other people and how to create chaos. Poppers and rockers do not get along, so why would Samantha and I be any different?

If you asked me a week ago, I would have described Samantha as a blonde, rich, hard-rock-loving villain who really wanted to ruin your life. Today I would describe her as a blonde, rich, hard-rock-loving human who just wants to be loved and accepted for who she is.

During this past week, I've done a lot of things that I never would have done if it was not for Samantha (both good and bad). I'm beginning to question what type of person I am and who I want to be in the future.

Gandhi once said, "Whenever you are confronted with an opponent, conquer him with love." Without thinking about it, I think both Samantha and I gave up on being enemies after day two of this experiment. It would not make the week go any faster by hating one another. Instead we just hung out, like I would with any other friend, and all of a sudden she became a person, not a 'rocker'.

Long Beach High is a sick place. We act like it's the first half of the twentieth century where black and white people are biological enemies, or Jews and the Nazis, or Pluto, Chip 'n' Dale. Of course I had been questioning our behavior earlier, but I've never really seen it through these moral *spectacles. To me, and probably many more, rockers were rockers, not humans with feelings and lives outside of school.*

Samantha can be really sweet and sensitive if she wants to and allows herself. She's very lonely, and I do feel kind of bad for her. She doesn't have any real friends, and her parents are rarely home. But her smile... I love seeing her smile. Maybe it is because I did not think she could ever be happy since I imagined her being angry all the time, or maybe it is because I feel sympathy for her, or maybe it is because I could be the one tiny reason for her smile.

If Samantha could have anything she wanted in this world, I'm sure she would ask for David Lee Roth to marry her, for her parents to love and accept her even if she does not go to Harvard or Stanford, and a bunch of new friends.

This is the hardest part of this experiment: what will be the results? I cannot predict the future. Will I and Samantha stay friends? If so, would the school allow us, or will it have to stay a secret? Could it change everything at LBH, or will it just fade into gray as time passes on? I can't say.

As she laid down her pen and leaned back against the chair where the sun heated up her face, the phone on her bedside table rang. It was so nice just resting her crazy head and overloaded body in the sun, but maybe it was something important. She decided to get up and answer it.

"Hello," she said.

"Hi, is this Clarice?" a male voice on the other end said.

"Yes, this is she."

"Hello, this is Tony speaking. Do you remember me from last night?"

Clarice remembered him more than well. He was Eye Candy's roadie wearing a Mets cap.

"Yes, I do. What do you want?" she asked.

"I'm calling on behalf of Mike, and he wants you to know that he is really sorry about the way he acted."

Clarice closed her eyes and sighed loudly as she started to massage her forehead with her fingers.

"And I guess you're calling cause he's lying all drunk in the back of the bus, unable to call me himself."

"Well," Tony hesitated.

"Just as I thought," Clarice said. "When he wakes up and gets all charmy again, you can tell him that I don't want him ever calling me again."

She immediately hung up the phone before Tony could add another word in Mike's favor and sat down on the side of her bed to take a few breaths. Inhale, exhale. She tried to kill off the screaming person inside of her and succeeded well enough to call Samantha.

"Harries's residence," Linda Harries said when answering the phone.

"Hello, it's Clarice. Is Samantha home?" Clarice asked, sounding a lot politer than when Tony called.

"Oh, hi, Clarice," Linda said. "I think she is in the kitchen. Let me get her."

Clarice looked herself in the mirror and saw two huge bags under her eyes as she waited for Samantha to pick up the phone. Did she even sleep at all this morning? Or had it just been a short nap?

"Hello," Samantha said.

"*Hola, ¿Qué estás haciendo*? Clarice asked, assuming Samantha could tell it was her by her voice.

The conversation paused, and the only thing Clarice could hear on the other end was some sort of crunchy noise.

"It means, *What are you doing*? Haven't you paid attention in Spanish class?" Clarice added to get the call back on track.

"I knew that," Samantha said. "I'm eating cereal. How about you?"

"Not much. Wanna grab some real food?"

"Drive-thru?"

Clarice's idea of 'real food' maybe was not the same as Samantha's, although who cared? Food was food.

"If I get to drive the Corvette."

"Fine," Samantha said, not sounding too happy. "I'll pick you up in twenty minutes." She hung up.

Clarice took the phone away from her ear and looked at it.

"Okay then," she said as she raised her eyebrows and

placed the phone back on the bedside table.

* * *

"Wow, you got a new car?" the drive-thru waitress asked as Clarice pulled up to order in Samantha's Corvette at Wendy's.

"Yeah, I got it last week," Clarice said with pride.

Sitting in the passenger's seat Samantha turned her head to Clarice with an expression like she had just heard the biggest betrayal ever. Although maybe she had. Clarice did, after all, claim to own her beloved car.

"Cool, now what would you like to order?" the waitress asked and corrected the Wendy's cap on her ginger-haired head.

"One salad, a burger with fries, and two peach ice teas please," Clarice said and took out her wallet to look for cash.

"And extra bags of ketchup," Samantha said while peeking out her head.

The waitress handed over the bag of food through the window to Clarice and accepted the cash in return. The bag filled the whole car with the smell of fast food burgers, and it made Clarice's stomach scream, even though she'd eaten breakfast not too long ago.

"Have a nice day," the waitress said with a bright smile on her berry lips.

"Thanks. You too," Clarice said as she pressed down the gas pedal and rolled away.

"Who was that?" Samantha asked as she opened the bag and put a French fry in her mouth.

Clarice looked to her left and right to make sure the coast was clear to make a left turn from the drive-thru.

"Her name is Penny," Clarice said. "She was in my dance class last year."

"Interesting. Now where should we eat?" Samantha asked.

Clarice looked around the area and took a right turn after the stop sign.

"Let's eat by the school," Clarice said with a smile and turned right onto the street where Long Beach High was located.

The school's parking lot looked so different, compared to a weekday when it was filled with cars in all the rainbow's colors and students running all over the place. Now it was calm, and the only ones playing on the sidewalks were the leaves in the wind. Clarice parked the car in the most popular parking space of them all; the one covered in shadow under the biggest palm tree. Samantha grabbed the bag with food and stepped out of the car. She then placed herself on the hood and looked at their empty school.

"What do you think about it?" she asked and got her burger out of the bag.

"The school?" Clarice asked. "Well, it's a bit old."

"Not the building, you idiot. I meant about going here."

Clarice giggled at Samantha's comment as she also got up on the hood and took out her food.

"I guess it's all right," Clarice said. "Why are you asking?"

"No, nothing special. I'm just thinking about tomorrow, after this unusual week."

"What do you think will happen?" Clarice asked.

"I don't know. I guess it will be just the same."

It was tragic to hear, but maybe Samantha was right. What could really change?

* * *

The soft sand played against the skin between Samantha's toes as she walked toward the white-painted beach chair located in the middle of the beach between her house and the wild ocean. It was a beautiful afternoon with great sunlight and cool winds from the sea. Samantha dusted the sand off the chair, sat down and opened her school notebook full of hateful comments about everything and everyone. There were only three blank pages left in the book, and she was to dedicate one of them to this week's assignment. She got out her pen and started by writing down her name at the top.

Samantha Harries

10/19/86

Week 42

I want to start this essay by saying that I really don't have to do this if I don't want to, because your threat about giving me suspension is not valid. My mother is a lawyer, and she says that only a principal can give a student suspension. Now you may say that you'll just tell the principal that you saw me smoking on school property and he will give me suspension, but did you really see me smoke? No. I did not even have a cigarette in my hand. Therefore, you have no reason to suspend me.

But since you seem to be so interested in me and Clarice, I will be nice and tell you a few things about her (who you did not see smoke either, btw).

1. *She is 17 years old and her birthday is April 13th (according to her driver's license).*
2. *She has not talked to her mom in over ten years.*
3. *She likes to work out and listen to Cyndi Lauper.*
4. *She hates romantic comedy movies.*
5. *She is a good listener.*

I have always known there was something special about Clarice. I just never knew what it was. The way she looks at people and the way she talks to them shows that she is just caring. And I haven't met many of her kind before.

I have no idea what she thinks or has written about me.

Hopefully, it is better than if we had written this during Monday's detention class. Although back then I wouldn't really have cared.

Clearly you wanted to do a Breakfast Club 2.0 on us, and yes, they all became friends in the end (obviously), but you never got to see what happened next. Did they go back to their old lives and old friends, or did they revolutionize the entire school? We'll never know.

But the truth is that this is not a John Hughes movie, and I really don't think Long Beach High School is ready for a Breakfast Club revolution. Nice try, though.

October 20, 1986

Standing by her locker, Clarice watched as Samantha communicated with her ex-boyfriend Chris and his friend James a bit further down in the hallway. It felt a bit odd seeing Samantha in their school environment again, almost like seeing your dad in a lingerie store or your best friend's little brother in your own room. A nice person in the wrong place.

"What are you looking at?" Amanda asked as she jumped up from behind Clarice alongside Andy and Teresa.

"What? No nothing," Clarice said and went back to digging in her locker.

"Has your cousin gone home now?" Teresa asked. "What was his name? Mick?"

Clarice remembered their little run-in on the beach promenade during the weekend and thought to herself that calling Mike her cousin from Chicago maybe was not the smartest idea since his face was on the cover of every magazine across the state.

"Don't you only have one cousin?" Amanda asked. "Who is a girl, by the way."

Clarice ignored Amanda's correct comment and looked back at Teresa.

"He traveled down to San Diego to visit some other relatives," Clarice answered in order to not say a complete lie since Mike actually was in San Diego on tour.

The clock had just passed 10am, and Clarice had been waiting for this moment the entire week. It was the deadline for their essays.

She took out her thin-lined paper and folded it into a small piece that fit in her pocket to not draw any attention from her friends standing close by.

"Are you ready?" Samantha asked as she showed up from nowhere in front of Clarice.

"Um, yeah," she said and closed her locker.

"Clarice?" Amanda asked from behind her as she walked away with Samantha toward Mr. Morgan's office.

"I'll be right back," Clarice said and gave Amanda a

gentle smile so she would not worry.

Even though she had spent the entire week with Samantha, all of a sudden it felt so wrong—what were they doing, walking alongside each other.

Besides their entrance at the Rainbow the other night, Clarice had never felt so observed as she did now. With their eyes practically falling out, the students of Long Beach High pressed themselves against the lockers as Clarice and Samantha walked down the hallway, and as soon as they entered Mr. Morgan's classroom, the students' mouths opened, popper to popper, rocker to rocker, whispers, screams, wordless sounds.

Inside Mr. Morgan's geography classroom, the air was cool from the fan spinning round and round on his messy desk with books, pens, and papers full of coffee stains.

"Well, well, if it isn't my favorite students," Mr. Morgan said with sarcasm as Samantha and Clarice walked in. "How was your week?" He crossed his arms while leaning back against his creaking chair.

"You'll have to find out in our essays," Clarice said.

"Fine," he said and reached out his hand to receive their papers.

Clarice and Samantha looked at each other before handing over their handwritten essays. Clarice had no idea what Samantha had written in hers, but she would never find out anyway, so why worry?

"Wait up a second," Mr. Morgan said as he saw how Samantha and Clarice headed back for the door they had come from. "Have you read each other's essays?"

"No," Clarice said, almost feeling as if she was accused of a crime.

"Then please sit down," he said and pointed at the beaches in front of him.

Samantha and Clarice looked with confused gazes at each other as they sat behind the exact same desks as last Monday during detention. In front of them, Mr. Morgan placed the other person's essay and told the girls to read them.

"What if I don't want to?" Samantha asked as she sounded sort of scared.

"Believe me: you have nothing to worry about," Clarice said. "But me on the other hand…"

"Just read the essays so you can move on to your other classes," Mr. Morgan said and put down his coffee cup with force on his desk.

Clarice sighed and looked down at the paper with Samantha's name written in the top right corner. She decided not to care if anything horrible was written, because unlike Samantha, Clarice at least had friends she cared about out in the hallway. She shook her head and started to read.

Samantha really did not want to read Clarice's text. What if she had been playing her the entire week and in reality hated Samantha. She did, after all, call her a bitch just this Thursday. She looked up at Mr. Morgan, who sighed when he saw that she did not read the paper as he'd told her to.

"Samantha," he said and pointed at the paper.

She looked over at Clarice, who had started to read. "What the hell," she thought and started to read the first sentence of Clarice's essay.

Clarice giggled as she finished Samantha's essay.

"You should really read this one, Mr. Morgan," she said and got up from her seat to give Mr. Morgan Samantha's paper.

"I will, but do you have something you would like to say to Samantha?" he asked and received the paper.

Clarice looked at Samantha who had just finished her essay and looked back up at Clarice with her almond-shaped green eyes and a smile on her lips.

"I think I said it all in the paper," Clarice said and shrugged as she looked back at Mr. Morgan.

"All right then. Thank you, girls. You can go now," Mr. Morgan said and put on his glasses to take a look at their essays.

In silence and with light steps, they walked out of the classroom and out to the hallway. As they opened the door, the loud students outside became quiet again.

"Was this all?" Clarice asked herself. A bunch of looks

and everybody going quite when you enter the hallway. Piece of cake. She and Samantha could easily be friends if this was the case.

"You were right," Samantha said. "That thing about my biggest wishes."

"And you were wrong about my birthday, it's April fourteenth, not thirteenth," Clarice said with laughter.

"Ouch," Samantha said. "Gonna have to write that in my calendar or something then so I don't miss out on it."

"Yeah, so what do you say? Do you wanna try it out?"

Samantha smiled to herself as she thought about what Clarice just asked.

"Well, I've never really cared what other people think of me before, so why start now?" she said.

"Good thinking," Clarice said and walked toward Amanda and Teresa, still standing by her locker.

She smiled at them, but they did not smile back. Instead, they turned around and started to whisper in each other's ears.

"Have you heard that our art class is canceled because Mr. Evans has the flu?" Clarice asked Samantha.

"No, that's cool," Samantha said. "Does that mean we can get out of here?"

"I guess so," Clarice said and looked around at the freaked out students she walked past.

At this moment, the main entrance appeared as a holy

gate to heaven in Clarice's mind, and she could hear the choir sing hallelujah as she got closer to it. Samantha grabbed the door handle with her right hand, and they faced the sunshine coming from right above.

Just as they were about to take their first step away from the school, they both got hit by something extremely cold. It was two seniors who felt the need to sacrifice their late breakfast smoothies to not see a popper and a rocker walking out of Long Beach High together, unharmed. With smashed blueberries all over their hair and body, Clarice and Samantha started laughing. They laughed at each other, with each other and at the school, they left behind.

Maybe Long Beach High was not ready for a change after all.

Or was it?

ABOUT THE AUTHOR

Being a late 90s kid, it is not easy to live a life, dreaming about what it would be like to have experienced the decade that defined the decades. Of course I'm talking about the 80s. So what do you do when you don't have a DeLorean and a few cans of plutonium just hanging around? Yeah, that's right, you write a book where you can experience your greatest desires though fictional characters.

Personally I was born in 1997 in Sweden of all places, and day dreaming has always been my specialty. I'm also a big killer whale lover and have a thing for palm trees in all its sizes.

I started writing this book in Febuary of 2015 on the train from my hometown to Stockholm. How J.K Rowling of me, right. And now you have it in your hands, or on your screen. It's been quite the journey, let me tell you that.

Feel free to contact me via my website or social media whenever, and use the hashtag #Week42 when talking about the book. Thank you so much!

www.ingramcontent.com/pod-product-compliance
Lightning Source LLC
Chambersburg PA
CBHW032212170626
46808CB00006B/2436

THE ISLES OF ABOTI

BOOK 3 OF THE SHAMRA

BY
LARRY HIGGINS

Published by True Beginnings Publishing.
Copyright by Larry Higgins, 2024.

ISBN-13: 978-1-947082-37-3

Ordering Information:
To order additional copies of this book, please visit Amazon.

The Isles of Aboti, Book 3 of The Shamra.
© Larry Higgins.
First Printing 2024.